WARWICKSHIRE
FOLK
TALES

T0347066

WARWICKSHIRE FOLK TALES

CATH EDWARDS

First published 2021

The History Press
97 St George's Place, Cheltenham,
Gloucestershire, GL50 3QB
www.thehistorypress.co.uk
© Cath Edwards, 2021

The right of Cath Edwards to be identified as the Author
of this work has been asserted in accordance with the
Copyright, Designs and Patents Act 1988.

British Library Cataloguing in Publication Data.
A catalogue record for this book is available from the British Library.

ISBN 978 0 7509 9315 9

Typesetting and origination by Typo•glyphix
Printed by TJ Books Limited

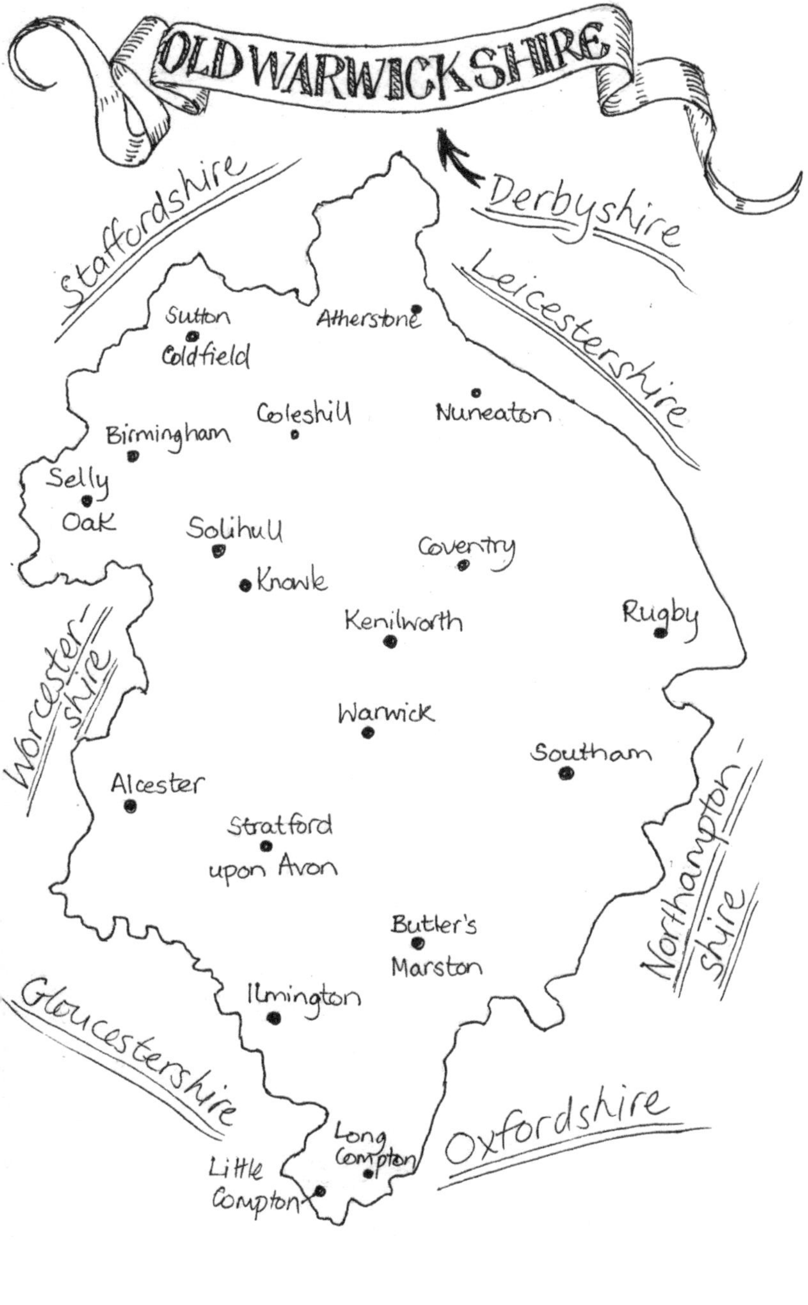

OLD WARWICKSHIRE

Staffordshire

Derbyshire

Leicestershire

Sutton
Coldfield

Atherstone

Coleshill

Nuneaton

Birmingham

Selly
Oak

Solihull

Coventry

Worcester-
shire

Knowle

Kenilworth

Rugby

Warwick

Southam

Alcester

Stratford
upon Avon

Northampton-
shire

Butler's
Marston

Gloucestershire

Ilmington

Long
Compton

Oxfordshire

Little
Compton

CONTENTS

INTRODUCTION

It has been such a pleasure to research and write these folk tales and legends. Warwickshire is a remarkable county: steeped deeply in England's history, its stories reflect the lives of the ordinary people who have called it their home as well as incidents from its warlike and heroic past.

In writing this book, I have learnt so much of the truth and fiction surrounding its most famous inhabitants: Godifu, or Lady Godiva; Guy of Warwick, who has heroic adventures to rival King Arthur, and with a conscience; and Saint George, who was, of course, born in Coventry. I found, also, an unexpected link between Saint George and Guy of Warwick; in some reports, George is Guy's father. Historically, that would put one or the other of them in the wrong century, in fact several hundred years awry, but when have the facts ever stood in the way of a story?

I have also uncovered stories of real people who had larger than life adventures: the fearless and reckless exploits of highwaymen and women, lamentable doomed lovers, the reputed dark deeds of real-life witches, courageous and tragic Civil War soldiers and even the redoubtable Saint Augustine.

This book has its fair share of the best-loved kinds of folk tales. So here you will find stories of witches and the supernatural, ghost stories and noodlehead (fool) stories.

As a storyteller, I love telling every kind of tale and equally as an author I love to include a variety of stories in my books. When I write, I usually write as a storyteller; what you will find in this book are my own versions of Warwickshire's stories, with something of the flavour of the way I would tell them to an audience. As anyone who is familiar with folkloric material will tell you, there are always different, sometimes contradictory, versions of the same story. Here are the versions that seemed to me to be the best and the best fit with the character and landscape of the county.

This brings me to another point: I have included stories from 'Old Warwickshire', that is, the Warwickshire with boundaries as they existed in past centuries, when, after all, these stories originated. When I was writing *West Midlands Folk Tales*, I deliberately left out stories from some of old Warwickshire, notably Coventry. It seemed to me that, even though that city is now included within the West Midlands county boundary, its stories, of Godiva and Saint George, really belong with Warwickshire, rather than in a county that has only existed since 1974!

If I may repeat myself, writing this book has been an absolute pleasure; I do hope you gain as much pleasure from reading it.

HIGHWAYMEN

DICK TURPIN

There are two little local tales concerning perhaps the most infamous highwayman of all. He has many legends attached to his name, and few, it would seem, are true. But veracity or the lack of it has never stood in the way of a good story. Let's look at the setting for one of these stories:

Stretton Baskerville has a sad history. The village, or what's left of it, lies between Leamington Spa and Hinckley, near to what is now the A5, known for centuries as the Roman road, Watling Street. In fact, 'Stretton' means 'settlement on a Roman road'. It's situated on a slope facing towards Leamington between the shallow valleys of two streams.

There is a record of the village being freely held by Edric the Wild before 1066. No doubt when Edric led English resistance to the conquering Normans, he had little time for the village, and after his time it passed through a number of hands, including William de Baskerville, who gave it his name.

Things began to change for the worse in the fifteenth century when Thomas Twyford, so that his sheep might safely graze, enclosed 160 acres of open field previously shared by the villagers, who observed ancient methods of strip farming. He destroyed seven of the villagers' houses into the bargain. The next owner, Henry Smyth, enclosed more land and would commit no expense to the maintenance of the remaining timber and clay houses and cottages, thus eventually rendering eighty people homeless. Even the church became a ruin and was used as an animal shelter.

So it was that by the eighteenth century, there was little of Stretton Baskerville left. The buildings were all but gone, leaving a series of earthworks: 'hollow ways' or sunken roads; raised, level rectangles that were the foundations of the former houses; the outlines of paddocks and gardens; saucer-shaped scoops near to the streams that had been ponds where bream were bred; and the remains of the cobbled main street. Thus, anyone who may have reason to want to bury an object in a place where it could easily be recovered would find plenty of landmarks in the ruins of Stretton Baskerville.

☙❧

Born in Essex in 1706, Dick Turpin did not confine his criminal activities to the south-east. His fabled ride from London to York in one day to establish an alibi was in fact undertaken by another highwayman, 'Swift Nick' Nevison, but nevertheless Turpin roamed the length and breadth of the country and it was in York that he met his end by hanging.

No coaching route was safe from his attentions; in Warwickshire, the mail coaches, passenger coaches and, of course, lone travellers who rode up and down Watling Street could all fall prey to an attack by Turpin.

One mild autumn afternoon, a coach and four was bowling merrily southwards, the Leicestershire countryside on the left of the road and Warwickshire's on the right. In the middle distance, for anyone who cared to look, were two or three small towns. There was a full complement of passengers and their luggage, roped precariously to the roof, rattled and bumped above their heads. The coachman was well wrapped up with his coat buttoned up to his chin, his hat pulled firmly down and a rug over his knees, for even on a mild afternoon it could be a chilly affair, sitting on the bench seat in the open. He noted Weddington Castle away to the south and congratulated himself on making good time from Derby.

He had drifted away into a reverie when he felt the coach slowing. He looked up to see a masked man on a black horse. The man was riding alongside one of the lead horses with a hand on the horse's bridle and he was twisted round in the saddle with a pistol trained on the coachman.

'Stop the coach!' said the man. He swept back his long black coat to reveal two more pistols pushed into his belt. The coachman hastened to do as he was commanded, making a show of pulling on the reins so the man could be left in no doubt of his co-operation.

Dick Turpin – because, of course, that is who he was – turned his horse and then reined it in alongside the coachman. Without a word, Turpin held out his hand and the other man gave him the reins. Turpin knotted them and dropped them out of the coachman's reach.

'Coachman! Why have we stopped?' called an angry voice. A man had his head sticking out of the window. Turpin levelled his pistol at the head and invited its owner to leave the carriage and to bring all his companions with him.

After a short pause, which was filled with frantic whispers, a hesitant little procession made its way down the coach steps and the passengers assembled on the road, huddled together as if for warmth.

Turpin wasted no time. 'I want your valuables. I want rings, bracelets, necklaces and gold coins. Anything small and expensive. Don't waste my time with silver.'

When no one moved, he pulled a second pistol from his belt. There was a sudden pulling off of gloves, a rummaging in pockets, a fumbling with necklaces, and soon there was a pile of glittering, glinting objects in the road.

Sliding down from his horse, Turpin flipped over the pile with the toe of his boot. 'I said no silver! And who put that purse there? Empty it!'

A young woman stepped forward and did as he had said. She took the opportunity to observe him more closely and she realised why he wanted only the smallest and most valuable items. The horse's saddlebags were so full the buckles were straining. Turpin's coat was heavy with the items that already filled its pockets. He hardly had space to take any more. She watched him as he stooped to scoop up the spoils, stuffing handfuls into his shirt.

Everyone watched in silence as he remounted and without a backward glance rode off towards the north-east.

Turpin rode for a short way then turned off the main road towards the Warwickshire side. He guided his horse along an overgrown lane, over a stream and up and over a low ridge. Stretton Baskerville. This was a good place, and it had been a good day, so good that he was reluctant to ride any further while carrying so much booty. Equally, it would be a mistake to arrive at an inn with his riches. He dismounted and led his horse through the remains of the village until he came to a spot that was both sheltered and easy to remember: just off the holloway, between the foundation plots of two houses, under a hawthorn tree. He found a sharp-edged stone that could serve as a shovel and began to dig. After a long time and much effort, the hole was big enough.

His hands sore and his shoulders aching, Turpin reached into one of the saddlebags and pulled out a sack, which he filled with most of his day's haul. He tied the top and dumped the sack into the hole, scraping the soil back in with the stone, then stamping it flat.

His plan, of course, was to return at a convenient time to retrieve his treasure. But he never did. He soon found it necessary to make his way to Yorkshire, where he assumed the name of John Palmer (his father's name was John and his mother's maiden name was Parmenter). After a year or two in Yorkshire, he was apprehended for the theft of two horses, a crime that carried the death penalty. He was hanged in 1739.

No more was heard of him on Watling Street for 180 years or so. Then, in the 1920s, a motorcyclist saw a strange sight approaching him out of the mist on that road. A man on a black horse, with a large black tricorn hat and a mask and wearing a coat with red sleeves rode towards the motorcyclist and then disappeared. There were a number of other sightings of Dick Turpin, reported in the local paper, and the red sleeves seem to be a recurring theme. Were people seeing what they expected to see? At about that time, a series of children's comics was published, entitled *The Dick Turpin Library*. Dick Turpin was shown wearing a black tricorn hat and a red coat.

Or, perhaps his ghost recalls the day he buried a sack full of loot at a ruined village and rode away.

ⱺ⧸ⱷ

Weddington Castle was mentioned in the previous story; the castle (or rather, it was a castellated manor house), was demolished in 1928 and a housing estate was subsequently built on the land. Nearby was Lindley Hall, described as a Palladian mansion and also sadly demolished, in 1925. In Dick Turpin's time though the hall would have been only twenty or thirty years old. It was reached by a half-mile-long drive from Watling Street and so, like Stretton Baskerville, it was within easy striking distance of the Roman road.

Lindley Hall was set in 94 acres of pastures and parkland and near to the hall was a hill, imaginatively titled the Mound. Towards the foot of the hill was a hole, now hard to find, but three centuries ago it was the entrance to a cave large enough to afford temporary living quarters to a man and a horse.

Dick Turpin, or so the story goes, when laden with gold and treasures from his adventures on Watling Street, would sometimes ride to the Mound and make his way into the cave, leading his horse behind him. Once inside he lit a lantern, which he set down on a large iron-bound chest. He reached into a secret pocket inside his coat and drew out three heavy keys. Moving the lantern to the floor to give better light, he knelt down and fitted a key into one of three locks on the chest; when each key had turned and each lock had clicked open, Turpin lifted the lid and peered inside, reassuring himself that the plunder was as he had left it. He now emptied his pockets and saddlebags into the chest, noting with some satisfaction how full it was becoming. He closed the lid and once again turned the three keys in their locks before using the chest as a seat on which to enjoy a meal of bread, cheese and beer that he had brought with him.

Soon afterwards, as in the previous story, Turpin found it expedient to flee to the North and such was the weight of the loot in the chest within the cave that he had no choice but to leave it, no doubt intending to retrieve it at a more convenient time.

It is here that events took a more supernatural turn. Before he left for Yorkshire, Turpin placed a guardian on the chest: a cockerel. This creature remained faithfully perched where the highwayman had left it until a man came with a key. How the man knew of the chest or the locks is not recorded but it may be sufficient to say that he was not just any man but an Oxford scholar and perhaps he was therefore privy to secrets that had eluded ordinary folk. He had one key, and it must have been a skeleton key because he placed it in the first lock and opened it; he placed it in the second lock and opened it; and he was just making an attempt on the third when the cockerel, inexplicably passive until now, attacked him and drove him from the cave.

The cockerel remained at his post, prepared to repel any marauders, and folklore has it that he will only yield if presented with one of Dick Turpin's bones. There is no record that this has come to pass, and so we must conclude that the cave, chest, cockerel and treasure are still in situ.

As a responsible author I feel I must point out that a very similar story is told of a hill known as Alcock's Arbour and a robber named Alcock, so it is just possible that a search for Turpin's cave may be a wasted journey.

&

Before we leave Dick Turpin, here are two more little anecdotes:

There are many old inns up and down the country that claim a link to the famous highwayman; one such is the Cock Inn in Sibson. The inn is on the Twycross Road to the north of Nuneaton and 3 or so miles north of Watling Street – very much in Warwickshire's 'Turpin territory'. The Cock Inn was built in 1250 and is a half-timbered building that still today

has a thatched roof. Turpin was said to have been a regular visitor; when he was being pursued by those intending to bring him to justice, he would hide his horse in the cellar while concealing himself in the bar chimney. The inn was also said to have a tunnel that ran the short distance from the inn to the village of Sibson: possibly another reason for an outlaw to take refuge there.

Finally, a return to Turpin's last days in York. When imprisoned and awaiting trial for horse theft, he wrote to his brother-in-law, Pompr Rivernall, in Essex, presumably asking for help. Although Turpin (at the time masquerading as John Palmer) was evidently allowed pen, ink and paper while in prison, it seems that he either did not have the correct money for the postage, or perhaps whoever posted the letter for him pocketed this extra cash. Whatever the reason, when the letter was delivered to Mr Rivernall he was asked to pay the cost of the postage. Seeing that it was marked as having been sent from York, he said that he knew no one in York and he refused to pay.

Perhaps Rivernall simply did not want to pay the charge, or perhaps he knew that his brother-in-law was in York and he was reluctant to be associated with him. There is no record of what Rivernall's wife, Turpin's sister Dorothy, thought about the matter. The letter was taken to the Saffron Walden office, where it was seen by a postal employee, James Smith. Smith recognised the handwriting and he took the letter to the local Justice of the Peace.

Smith explained to the judge that before working for the post office he had been a schoolmaster and he had taught many boys to write. The handwriting on the letter was, he was sure, that of one of his former pupils, by the name of Richard Turpin. The judge, having first scrupulously paid the postage, opened the letter and read it. Although Turpin had not signed it in his own name, the contents made it clear who he was. The judge sent word to York, and Turpin, unmasked, had to stand trial for his many violent crimes as a highwayman.

On his way to the gallows and wearing a stylish new outfit he waved regally to the throngs of people, giving every impression of enjoying the crowd's attention and the stir he was causing. He was hanged but he had lost nothing by having his true identity revealed: the penalty for horse theft was also death by hanging.

BENDIGO MITCHELL

The Black Horse Inn can be found in Warwick town centre. As you stand and look at it from the other side of the road, on its left side are large wooden double doors typical of old coaching inns. It was formerly painted with a depiction of the highwayman Bendigo Mitchell, mounted on a black horse with a white blaze and four white socks, holding up a coach. A woman's arm extends from the coach window towards Mitchell, holding a drawstring pouch, presumably containing valuables. Red-coated attendants on the coach have their hands raised in surrender.

A plaque on the doors read:

> Bendigo Mitchell was an eighteenth-century highwayman. He plied his trade on the Warwick turnpike and waylaid those who had enjoyed a profitable trade at Warwick market. He rode 'Skater' – named after an icy escape from imminent arrest. Eventually captured, he was tried at Warwick Assizes in 1776 and publicly hanged across the road at the top of what is now the Sainsbury's car park.

Mitchell's unusual first name is thought to be a corruption of 'Abednego'. The parish records at Harbury show an Abednego Mitchell who died in 1852; this Abednego is believed to be a member of the same family as Bendigo.

Bendigo Mitchell, as the pub plaque suggests, did indeed work the Warwick to Banbury turnpike, as well as the Fosse Way. He is remembered still: locally, the intersection near Harbury is known as 'The Bendigo Mitchell Crossroads'.

Here is the story of Mitchell's 'icy escape from imminent arrest'.

Bendigo Mitchell was having a profitable day. He had held up two coaches and had relieved the passengers of their valuables, but one coach in particular had been carrying several rich people with a good amount of gold on their persons. He considered: should he repair to the inn for refreshment and the warmth of a log fire, it being a cold January day? Or should he spend one more hour lying in wait for others who were travelling on Fosse Way that day? He had come to no firm conclusion when he saw four men approaching. They were all on horseback, and Mitchell had started to debate with himself whether the odds were too much against him – four against one – when he began to feel uneasy. Something didn't look right. It was more about what the men weren't than what they were. They didn't look at all like local farmers; the horses were wrong, too racy and spirited. They didn't look like merchants; they carried no goods. They weren't travellers, not on those horses and with no baggage.

What were they, then, but constables sent from Warwick to apprehend criminals who worked these roads? Mitchell's suspicions were confirmed when, turning his horse's head away from the men and urging it into a canter, he looked behind him to see that the four had increased their speed too and were gaining on him. He thought quickly; ahead was the turning for Windmill Hill Lane. That would lead to Plough Lane where he could turn left, and that would take him back to Fosse Way and the way home. If he could outrun the constables.

At full gallop now, he left Fosse Way, turning sharp left. Windmill Hill Lane. He galloped on for half a mile or so. The men were still gaining on him. What to do? He would never gain Fosse Way, he had to escape another way. He saw ahead a narrow drive leading off to the right. He could ride up to Chesterton Mill, leap the hedge behind it and lose himself in the length of a few fields.

By the time Mitchell was galloping up the drive, the four constables were closing fast. The hoofbeats on the frozen ground sounded dangerously close. The mill buildings were just ahead now – but as he rode into the mill yard, he saw that the gap he thought he could ride through was far too narrow. He turned to face his pursuers like a fox at bay. They had reined in their horses and were waiting in the drive. Mitchell was outnumbered but still he was dangerous. Seconds passed.

Mitchell's heart thundered in his chest. Time for desperate measures. He drew his pistol and walked his horse towards his pursuers, watching their faces. He suddenly spurred his horse on, guiding it around the end of the mill towards the millpond. The constables watched him with some interest. What would he do when he found his escape completely barred by the pond?

Mitchell paused only for a moment at the edge of the frozen pond. No time to gauge the thickness of the ice. Maybe better to die this way, a free man. Forward once more, over the pond, the horse's hooves sliding dangerously. A loud crack that he thought was a pistol shot was but the ice breaking. Onwards, the ice near to giving way with each step, almost at the bank now – and the horse scrambled on to firm ground. Mitchell looked back. The constables were at the far side of the pond, not daring to follow. He rode through the barely-flowing Tach Brook, keeping up the pace, knowing they would be looking for a way to head him off. South to Chesterton Green – the country too open for his liking – then he found the relative seclusion of a lane. He followed it to Chesterton Wood. Here he waited for an hour or more until he was sure his pursuers had given up the search, then he made his way towards the warm and friendly inn.

When he told the story of his escape to his friends, the horse gained a new name: Skater.

☙❧

Chesterton Mill is still there, off Windmill Hill Lane. It's a Grade II listed building.

Bendigo Mitchell is no more. As the plaque on the pub door suggests, he was tried at Warwick Assizes in Northgate Street and publicly hanged just down the hill next to the racecourse.

Two recent online correspondents have added further information. Wiggerland Wood Farm now seems to have been given over to a housing development, but in the 1990s there was a plaque in a barn there that stated that Bendigo Mitchell was lynched in that same building. Further, it is said that the *Rugby Advertiser* of 26 November 1904 carried a report that Mitchell was hanged at Rugby and gibbeted at Warwick. Where is the truth I wonder?

A HIGHWAYWOMAN

At the time of writing, Stratford-upon-Avon hosts a farmers' market in Rother Street. It's on the first and third Saturdays of the month, if you're interested, and it also has stalls offering new goods, old goods, vintage and rare items, jewellery, hand-made crafts and lots more.

In centuries past, Rother Street, Bridge Street and Wood Street were the principal locations for the annual fairs that brought hundreds of people to the town. There was a hiring fair, where servants looking for work would fix small tokens of the employment they sought to their clothes or their head-dress: a groom carried a whip; a farm labourer a twist of hay; a shepherd a wisp of wool; and a maid-of-all-work a mop (hence 'mop fair'). The servants would be taken on for a year and a day.

The street sufficed as a cattle market, and beasts were tethered to iron rings fixed firmly into the walls; Rother Street still had some of these rings remaining until just over a hundred years ago.

In the week or so before the fair, the borough constable collected contributions from the public to buy a hog to roast. There must have been some sort of ticketing system for the contributors to claim their share of the profits. A sixteenth-century half-timbered inn, now The Garrick in the High Street, would roast the whole hog outside the front of its premises and plates of the meat were sold to passers-by, super-intended by the constable.

Stratford was full of people with money to spend and people with goods to sell. At the day's end, the pockets of the farmers and other traders would be heavy with coin. Some stayed at one of the several inns in the town to celebrate a good day making money by spending some of it, while those who lived more locally made their way home at the end of their day's trading. Farmers who lived to the south would ride their horses or drive their carts along Bridge Street, across the Avon bridge and into the Banbury Road. Some carried straight on, others soon turned right into the Shipston Road.

There was a woman who I will call Moll living 5 miles south of Stratford in the tiny village of Wimpstone. Moll led a double life. By day she was the quiet woman who kept herself to herself, looking after her vegetable garden and her chickens and occasionally bartering a few eggs or a cabbage or some onions for the necessaries of life. By night, when the time was right, she became something quite different.

On the Stratford fair days, Moll would wait for sunset. Then she went up to her bedroom and began to prepare herself. Her skirt she cast off in favour of a pair of well-worn breeches. She pulled on a pair of high black boots. She reached into the furthest recess of her cupboard to find a long, black, brass-buttoned coat, a three-cornered hat and a mask. She put them all on, looking in her cracked and spotted mirror as she adjusted the hat to its most rakish angle. Finally she reached an arm under her bed and drew out a pair of pistols, which she stuck into her belt.

She skipped light-footed down the stairs and into the kitchen, where she took a bridle from its hook. Out of the back door, she ran down the garden to the fence below. This she climbed, and gave a low whistle. Almost at once, the neighbouring farmer's black hunter trotted up and nuzzled her hands. She had him well trained. Any carrots she could spare from her garden were saved for him and he had learnt the meaning of the whistle. She soon had the bridle over his head and had climbed from the fence on to his bare back.

A gate took Moll from the field on to the village street, and she was away, cantering through the gathering darkness towards Stratford.

A farmer who lived 3 or so miles south of Stratford had had a good day. All the goods he had brought with him that morning were sold: cider, cheeses, a few fleeces and wooden boxes full of vegetables. He had met two old friends as he was packing up his stall and the three of them repaired to an inn for refreshment.

One of the friends said, 'We were in the High Street and we fancied a bit of something to eat, so we had a plate each of that meat they were roasting. The constable was there and he gave us a very useful tip about travelling towards Shipston.'

The other friend nodded. 'Yes, apparently there's been some trouble on that road. Often after these fairs.'

Now all three were travelling together, the farmer in his cart and the two friends on their horses. They were about 3 miles from Stratford on the Shipston Road, the moon three-quarters full, when they heard hoofbeats. Approaching them along the road was a dark-clad figure on a tall horse. When about twenty paces away, the figure reined in the horse and pulled something out of its belt. A gun barrel gleamed dully in the moonlight.

'Give me your money!' The voice was gruff.

The farmer's friends both reached under their coats and took out their own pistols.

'No, I don't think we will!' said one.

Moll said no more but turned her horse's head towards home and urged him on. Encouraged by this small victory, the two friends and the farmer gave chase. Or at least, the two men galloped after Moll, while the farmer in his cart managed to induce his horse to break into a trot.

Moll leaned low over the horse's neck. She congratulated herself for borrowing an excellent mount and she almost laughed with the exhilaration of moving at such speed. The men behind her could not match her pace, but they could see in the dim moonlight that she had taken the Wimpstone Road. Now she was crossing the little bridge over the Stour, now she'd turned into the village main street.

The men reined in their horses at the edge of the village. They were sure she had come this way, but they seemed to have lost her. Then one of them saw a movement at one of the houses some hundred yards away. Someone was entering a front door – but which one?

Moll closed the door behind her and lifted the heavy bar into place. The horse, back in his field, was still wearing the bridle but she would have to retrieve it at first light. Had she been seen? She thought she'd caught sight of the two men as she'd entered the house. Quick! She dragged off the coat as she ran upstairs and threw it into the cupboard with the hat and mask. There was the thud of heavy knocking at the front door. She grabbed her nightgown and flung it over her head, scrabbling for the armholes. Thudding again from the door, then silence.

She looked out of her window: the back garden, the chicken coop, washing flapping lazily on the line. All quiet. Then movement and whispered voices:

'See if we can get in this way.'

'Are you sure this is the right house?'

'Not really but we'll find out, won't we?'

With a thrill of fear, Moll recalled leaving the house by the back door. Had she locked it? She couldn't remember but she had her answer when she heard men's voices inside the house followed by footsteps on the stairs.

She yanked back the counterpane, jumped into bed and pulled the covers up to her chin. The footsteps ascended, slowing as they neared the top. A hurried, urgent conversation outside her door then it burst open and two men strode in.

Moll did not hesitate. She knew the only defence remaining to her. She screamed, loud and long, the piercing wail only broken when she drew breath in order to shriek anew.

The men appeared pinned to the spot. They stared, round-eyed at this terrible banshee they had, as they thought, awoken. Then they started to protest their innocent intent, to back away, to apologise over and over. They turned and ran down the stairs and Moll, after checking from the window that they had really retreated, went down and secured the back door.

In her bedroom once again, she sat on the bed. If they had cared to look, they would have seen the pistols where they had fallen to the floor. She nudged them with her foot. They were empty, as always. She slid them under the bed. And if they had dared to pull back the covers … She laughed to herself as she bent to pull off her high riding boots.

SAINT AUGUSTINE IN LONG COMPTON

SAINT AUGUSTINE

Augustine, in the days when he was plain Augustine with no hint of sanctity, was the Prior of the Abbey of Saint Andrew in Rome. Gregory, whom we know as Pope Gregory, was the Abbot. Thus Gregory was the titular head and Augustine did the work.

Perhaps it was Augustine's opinion that this state of affairs was set to continue when Gregory ordered him to England to convert King Aethelberht to Christianity. This was the way things were done in the sixth century; rather than trying to win round the populace one man or woman at a time, if the missionary could persuade the ruler to change his, and it almost always was a 'his', religion, then the rest of the populace would follow suit. Thousands for the price of one.

This Anglo-Saxon pagan Aethelberht was not such a tough nut to crack as you might think. Firstly, his wife was the Princess Bertha, daughter of the King of Paris; not only was she a Christian, but she was allowed to practice her faith with her own church and her own bishop. Secondly, Christianity in England already had a long history. The Romans had brought Christianity to Britannia, though the later invading Saxons rather trampled it underfoot. Thirdly, Pope Gregory had prepared the way with a number of letters to the Christian Franks (think French) asking for their support.

Aethelberht was the King of Kent. This may not sound very grand, but in those days, when the fastest means of travel was on the back of a horse, the land would have seemed much larger. And this king was the foremost in Britain; the Venerable Bede, in his later chronicles of English history, notes that Aethelberht had imperium, or overlordship, of all the land south of the Humber. Happily for Gregory, Aethelbert's coastal kingdom was also very conveniently reached from a Channel crossing.

Forty companions, some of them monks, were found for Augustine for this missionary journey. They set out from Rome, leaving behind the home they knew, the warm and sunny weather, the good food and drink and their friends and families. They turned their faces towards a colder, bleaker and probably hostile land. Not long after leaving Rome this good company began to get cold feet. At first there were murmurings; these were followed by mutterings, then outright dissent in the ranks. A deputation was sent to speak to Augustine. In short, they didn't want to go. Whether Augustine agreed openly is not recorded, but actions speak louder than words, and the action that he took was to return to Rome and to consult with Gregory. Was this trip really necessary?

We will never know the details of the conversation between the two men, but it would seem that Augustine was sent back to complete his journey with the Roman equivalent of a flea in his ear.

Eventually, then, the missionary company landed on the Kent shore, from where they made their way to the king's seat in Canterbury. It seems the conversion was rapid, and indeed only a year or so after travelling to Britain, on Christmas day 597, Augustine held a mass baptism of thousands of Aethelberht's subjects. By the year 598, Pope Gregory recorded in a letter that 10,000 British people had been baptised Christians.

Perhaps buoyed up by this success, Augustine, the first Archbishop of Canterbury, continued to extend his influence as the years passed. Two areas eluded him: Dumnonia (roughly today's Devon, Cornwall and Somerset) and Wales, where the Christians were quite happy to carry on in their own way. Some might say that those areas are still characterised today by independence and a strong sense of self. Nevertheless, Augustine gained the epithet 'Apostle to the English'.

It is doubtful that he carried out much missionary work in person; he founded a school to train others to carry out such duties. But there is a lovely story of him visiting the church at Long Compton while on one of his journeys – and here it is.

In Saint Augustine's time, Long Compton church was already ancient. There was said to have been a church and a parish priest there from before the time of the Saxons, so it must have been Roman in origin. The building was made of stone to a simple design but it bore a cross and that was all that mattered to the priest and to the people.

In those long-ago days, there was no central fund to pay for
the appointment of the priest. The custom was for the people
to pay tithes, that is one tenth of their monetary income or
of their harvest according to the trade they followed. The

money thus gathered paid for the upkeep of the church
and the stipend of the priest so that the spiritual needs of
the community were catered for. There was somewhere to
worship, somewhere to pray, somewhere to be christened,
somewhere to be married and somewhere and someone to
conduct the due ceremony when the time came to pass on to
a better life. A better life for most.

The day came when little Long Compton was to be visited by the great man himself, Bishop Augustine. The bishop was conducted by the priest on a brief tour of the village, meeting some of the residents, then the two men repaired to the priest's lodgings to discuss parish matters. Before long, the priest, quite possibly relieved to have someone with whom to share his concerns, got on to the subject of tithes.

'Of course,' said the priest, 'the people all pay faithfully, in one way or another, a tenth of their income. That is, almost all.'

Augustine waited for him to go on.

'It saddens me to report,' the priest said at length, 'that one on whom I would hope to rely to set a good example in fact does the opposite. The lord of this place, and a knight of the realm, refuses to pay anything at all. I have pleaded with him, cajoled him, I have even resorted to threats concerning his immortal soul, all to no avail. For the sake of the others, I have had to excommunicate him, for why should the honest share their church and their worship with one who will not contribute?'

Augustine nodded. 'And where might this knight be found?'

The priest told him, and Augustine set out alone to confront this unholy man.

When the knight's servant had admitted Augustine to the manor house, and the knight himself entered the room where the bishop was waiting, if he was surprised, he gave nothing away. The bishop's costly clothing, his authoritative bearing and his grave expression were all in contrast with the priest who used to call on the knight.

Augustine's first words were to the point. 'I understand that the priest has had to excommunicate you for repeated failure to pay the tithes that are due.'

The knight's cheeks coloured, but he kept his gaze steady. 'I have told the priest many times, and now I will tell you. I plough the land, or anyway, I have it ploughed. I have the seed broadcast, and I see the rooks and crows stealing three-quarters of that seed for which I have paid. I have my men reap the corn and tie it into sheaves. I have to pay for the feeding, clothing and lodging of these workers. No one gives me anything and any profit from the land is due to my good management. The tenth sheaf is as much mine as the other nine. Now, and I'm asking you politely, you had better leave before I lose my temper.'

Augustine nodded and began to make his way out of the room. With his hand on the door, he turned back to the knight. 'I will be leading mass in the church tomorrow morning,' and with his apparently pointless comment hanging in the air, he left.

After the bishop had gone, the knight set to thinking. Why had he mentioned the mass? Was there some significance? Would something special happen at the service? He had an answer for none of these questions, and the more he thought, the more intrigued he became.

The next morning, Augustine was indeed in the rough old pulpit, and the faithful were all seated in rows, gazing up expectantly. Before the bishop could begin, the outside door slammed open and the knight stalked in, glared at anyone with the temerity to look round at him and sat at the back of the church.

Augustine merely gave a brief nod to the newcomer, and began in a clear, firm voice: 'We will celebrate mass together. But first, let anyone who has been excommunicated leave this church!'

For a long moment, there was silence. Then the knight, his face a picture of glowering petulance, began to rise to his feet. Once standing, he clutched wildly for the back of the pew in front of him at the same time as the congregation gasped. The stone floor had begun to tremble and there was a low grating rumble as, inch by inch, a huge slab lifted.

With a thunderous boom, the slab fell aside and everyone stared into the fissure beneath. A grey, shrivelled hand appeared, the fingertips feeling along the edge of the stone as if searching for a handhold. It found a crack and gripped it, pulling hard. A head rose out of the ground, the eyes sunken, the hair sparse, but strangely, around its neck was a gold chain. The body continued to heave itself out of its grave, first falling to its knees on to the church floor, then rising unsteadily to its feet.

It was the corpse of a man, richly dressed and looking very dead.

The man turned his sad face to Augustine and said in a voice like the tearing of old parchment, 'I will go.' He began to shuffle towards the door, past the horrified knight. Augustine hastened down from the pulpit and laid a hand on the dead man's arm.

'Stay,' he said. 'Tell me, what is your story?'

'Long, long ago, I was the lord over this place. I had fields to work and men to work them. The priest asked me many times to pay tithes. I would not. I was excommunicated, and that is how I died. Since then,' he seemed lost in thought for a time. 'Since then, I have been in hell.'

'Where is he now?' asked Augustine. 'That priest, where is he?'

The man lifted a grey hand and pointed out of the door towards the churchyard. Haltingly, he began to move, the bishop and the knight following.

This strange procession made its way out of the church and among the gravestones until the man stopped before an old worn stone under the shade of a yew tree.

'He lies here.'

Augustine stepped to the head of the grave, and said in a commanding voice, 'Arise, priest, arise, for we now have need of you.'

The knight felt himself gripped with a horrified fascination as the surface of the grave first shivered, then heaved and lurched, then finally, with rather more energy than had the first corpse, the old priest pulled himself out of his grave. He stood erect and, making no effort to conceal his annoyance, said, 'Who summoned me?'

Augustine was just opening his mouth to admit to the deed, when the priest's gaze fell on the dead man. 'You! I might have known it! Dead for a hundred years and more, and still making my life difficult!'

The dead man fell to his knees and offered up the most heartfelt and passionate confession of all his sins. This took some time.

The old priest's expression softened. 'Ah well, better late than never.' He gestured over the man's head. 'I absolve you of all wrongdoing. You may pass on to another life of peace and joy.'

The knight and Augustine heard a sound like a rusty saw drawn through hard timber. They looked at each other, then both realised what it was. The dead man was sobbing. Augustine gently helped him to his feet, and said, 'You may go.' The man mumbled thanks to the bishop and the priest and he shambled back into the church, whence came a grating roar as, the listeners surmised, the stone had replaced itself above the man's corpse.

'And now,' said Augustine brightly as he turned to the old priest, 'would you like me to offer up prayers so that you may be returned to life on earth and thus have the opportunity to save more sinners from hell?'

'No,' was the answer. 'I would not. Kindly leave me be.' The priest turned his back and wriggled his way back into his grave and back to paradise.

'Well then, that just leaves you.' Augustine turned to the knight with a smile.

The knight was visibly trembling. 'I'll pay, I'll give the church everything I owe. I need to confess my sins too, there's more, there's much more.' He too, like the old lord, fell to his knees.

'I'm sure you do,' said Augustine. 'I have a feeling we will need to sit in comfort. Let's go inside.' He led the knight back into the church, where the congregation, astonished and aghast, had not moved.

The knight did confess, but that was not all. He sold his lands and gave the money to the church. He became a monk and eventually a follower of Saint Augustine. He took to walking the highways and lanes of Mercia, travelling from village to village, from town to town, preaching, for the rest of his earthly life, to any and all who would listen.

THE ROLLRIGHT STONES AND WITCHES IN LONG COMPTON

THE LEGEND OF THE ROLLRIGHT STONES

This legend straddles the border between Warwickshire and Oxfordshire; some of the elements it concerns are geographically in the more southern county.

> The common people usually call them the **Rolle-rick** stones and dreameth that they were sometimes men by a wonderful metamorphosis turned into hard stones.
>
> Camden's *Britannia*, 1586

The Rollright stones comprise: The King's Men, a circle of about seventy stones (more on this later); The King Stone, a lonely monolith from which Long Compton cannot be viewed as it is obscured by the hilltop; and The Whispering Knights, a portal dolmen to a former burial chamber.

The tale as most often told today is based on a work published in 1895 by Sir Arthur Evans and tells of an invading army led by a king; he is confronted by a witch who says:

> Seven long strides shalt thou take,
> And if Long Compton thou canst see,
> King of England thou shalt be.

The king begins his seven strides, saying:
Stick, stock, stone!
As King of England I shall be known!

But the ground rises up as he takes his final step, obscuring his view of Long Compton in the valley below.

The witch then says:

As Long Compton thou canst not see
King of England thou shalt not be.
Rise up, stick, and stand still, stone,
For King of England thou shalt be none.
Thou and thy men hoar stones shall be
And I myself an eldern tree.

And so it was.

※

My own version is based on earlier legends, and here it is.

The sea voyage had been tedious and longer than any of the party, from the humblest foot soldier to the king, had expected. Sharing a boat with horses, none of whose four legs was of the sea variety, and which therefore expressed their ill feeling frequently and copiously, was a trial. The sea had splashed up and the rain had lashed down. Food and water were rationed and, towards the end of the journey, far from fresh. The landing on the south-eastern corner of Britain was a relief.

Since death in battle conferred on the fallen a glorious and rumbustious afterlife, no Norseman feared it, and yet it was not easy for a man to see his son, his brother, his friend cut down before him. The small army had met with resistance from the moment they had set foot on land. The first was a little group of frightened villagers who had given their lives to protect their own, but not before they had mortally wounded two of the Danes.

And that had been the way of it. Slogging along on foot, following the king and his five noblemen as they rode, suffering surprise attacks which they always repelled but which always took their toll. Making their way mile after mile across a hostile land, day by day losing men, and for what? The king, the men knew, was intent on conquering the land and crowning himself its king. The men had also observed something to which the king seemed oblivious.

The noblemen, in the early days, had ridden ahead of the army with the king. But as time had passed, they had taken to splitting off and falling behind. One or two of them would ride alongside the king, talking earnestly with him about matters that the soldiers could only guess at. The others, on the pretext of chivvying or encouraging the men on foot, would drop back and have little conversations of their own: whispered words spoken without looking at one another. The foot soldiers, accustomed as they were to sharing and handing over watches through the night, could see that the noblemen had a similar system in play. Never was the king left alone. Always one or two of his retinue, different men each time, would be alongside him while the others whispered to each other behind.

The army, small to begin with but even smaller now that many minor battles had taken their toll, began to lose heart. They numbered little more than seventy men, and it looked as though their leader's hope of self-glorification was a vain one.

They were all brave men and fierce fighters, but now that they were unsure even of the noblemen's allegiance their faith in their leaders was fading.

One morning in early summer, a lark high overhead sang with piercing sweetness. The king called all of his men together. Under their feet, the arrowhead leaves of sorrel gave off a sharp scent. The king began. 'I have something of great importance to tell you. I have spent the night considering the runes, and they tell me that a thousand years from now, people will still be telling my story. This must mean that my destiny is to be realised and I am to be crowned king of this land.'

He paused, nodding sagely. 'Just over this hill,' he swept an arm behind him, 'there lies a village. Long Compton is its name. Beyond the village is the whole of the rest of Britain. My land, and your land. Come! I will ascend to top to view my kingdom!'

The king turned and began to walk up the hill, the army straggling behind him, the noblemen drifting away a little. A buzzard wheeled overhead.

The distance increased between the men and their leader. He was nearing the top of the hill. Perhaps seven strides, he judged. As he strode closer and closer still, he was brought up short. A man had appeared on the skyline, just above the king. His eyes were pale and piercing. With a glance he took in the king, the ragged army and the five nobles, now a little distance to the east.

'Who are you, to set foot on my land and my people's land?' The pale-eyed man addressed the king.

The Dane eyed the Anglo-Saxon with undisguised scorn. 'Step aside. I and my army wish to enjoy a view of the land that is soon to be mine!'

'That you shall never see.' The Anglo-Saxon was assured. He glanced over his shoulder and in a moment he was joined on the hilltop by scores of men, long-haired, pale-eyed, standing shoulder to shoulder, blocking any hope of a view of the valley beyond. They drew their swords.

The king turned, in a panic, to seek the protection of his nobles but they were too distant to be of any help. His army was away further down the hill. He stood alone and he stands there still.

As the Anglo-Saxons surged down the hill, the king's army hastily tried to form a defensive circle and the nobles huddled closely together. None survived; or in a way they all did, since there they remain.

Whether it was witchcraft or the old magic of the Britons we cannot know, but the evidence of what happened on that day is there still for anyone to see. The king, turned to stone, is near the top of the hill and alone. The army are now a stone circle. His noblemen, the 'Whispering Knights', stand in a cluster and are whispering still. Whatever treason they were plotting against their king is now frozen in time forever more.

☙

As to how many men were left in the army on that fateful day, that is hard to say; the stone circle is reputed to be uncountable. Once, a Long Compton baker tried. He filled a basket with small loaves and set off up the hill to the stone circle. He walked around the circle, placing one loaf at the foot of each stone. Halfway round, he realised that he had not counted the loaves to begin with. He retraced his steps, replacing the loaves in the basket, then sat down to count them. He set off again.

One loaf for each stone. Three-quarters of the way round he ran out of loaves.

He set off back to his bakery to collect some more. Part-way down the hill towards the village it occurred to him that if he left the first batch of loaves in the stone circle, wild animals or birds or worse, local children, might make off with them. He turned and trudged back up the hill, collected up the loaves and carried them down to his bakery. Once there he had a bit of a sit down. While he was resting, a thought came to him. He didn't need more loaves. He could tear the ones he already had in half. He emptied the basket on to the floor, refilling it with half loaves.

He laboured up the hill again, marvelling at the fact that tearing loaves in half could make them heavier. At last, he was back at the circle. An elder tree stood just outside its perimeter, and the baker stared very hard at it. How could an elder tree smirk? He wasn't sure, but there was a definite sneering smugness about its demeanour. He chose to rise above the implied taunt and carry on with his task.

One half loaf to every stone. How hard could it be? Halfway round he realised he hadn't counted the half loaves. He began to collect the loaves back into the basket and he was nearly back at the start when it dawned on him that the number of half loaves would be double the number of whole loaves, which he had earlier counted. He tried to remember the original number. This necessitated another sit down and a good scratch of his head. At last, he remembered the number and doubled it, then resumed the placement of loaves.

This time, he managed to get all the way round the circle. He knew this because the moment came when he was about to place a loaf at the foot of a stone and he found that the stone already had one. Now, all he had to do was count the number of half loaves he had left and subtract that number from the total number of half loaves that he started with, then he would know how many stones there were in the circle.

For one glorious moment, he thought he had achieved his goal. Then a sudden cold feeling washed over him. He had overlooked one thing. He had counted the whole loaves before he set off back to his bakery, then, judging it unwise to leave them there, he had gone back for them. What if, in the intervening time, a fox or a crow or a child or all three had taken a loaf? That would put out his calculations.

If this was a folk tale, he would be there still, endlessly counting and recounting, picking up and replacing his increasingly battered half loaves. But instead, he looked to the west where a glorious sunset was setting the sky aflame, and his thoughts turned to his fireside, a good supper and a comfortable bed. He tipped out the contents of the basket and went home.

This does not answer the question, how many were left in the army and thus, how many stones are in the circle? Some people have counted seventy-one. Some people have counted seventy-four. It's a lovely spot. Why not try it for yourself?

౿〇౿

There are a few more little tales about the stones. One is about a farmer who had a problem with a stream that ran along the edge of his farmyard. In summer, he could step across it but in winter it swelled and froze and was a lot more tricky to navigate. One day, when he was walking past the

Rollright stones, he looked anew at the group of large rocks known as The Whispering Knights. One of them was long and wide and flattish and it seemed to the farmer that it would be ideal to lay across the stream from bank to bank; it would easily create a bridge. He hurried back to his farm and called for John, the man who laboured for him.

Now, the farmer considered John not to be the cleverest of men, but he was a good worker and he generally did as he was asked. This day, the farmer told John to harness the two plough horses and bring them, with some strong rope, up the hill to where the old stones were. John looked doubtful but he did as he was told.

When they arrived at the stones, the farmer pointed out the stone he wanted and he told John to secure the horses' traces to the stone with the rope so they could pull it down.

John did not move. 'I don't think you want to do that,' he said.

The farmer was not accustomed to being contradicted. 'How do you know what I want? Now do as I say!'

John still hesitated, but no doubt realising that he could lose his job if he disobeyed, he wound the rope around the stone and tied it to the harness. Reluctantly, and muttering to himself, he began to lead the horses down the hill. The rope tightened, the horses leaned into their collars and strained, but nothing happened.

The farmer was perplexed. He sent John to call on their neighbour's farm with a request to borrow their horses. John sloped off, grumbling about things that 'just shouldn't be done'. He did, though, eventually return with the neighbour's horses. These two were roped to the stone alongside the farmer's two horses and all four pulled. No movement.

John was sent to the neighbouring farm on the other side. He grumbled again, this time that 'someone is trying to tell us something', but again he did as he was told and again returned with two more horses. This time, with six big plough horses harnessed to the stone, it began to move, grudgingly and slowly. It took all the horses' effort to drag the stone downhill to the farm and then to slide it into place across the stream.

The farmer was triumphant. 'There, John, what's the matter with you? It's perfect, now we've got a bridge.'

John did not reply. He simply turned and led the four borrowed horses back to their owners.

That night, the family in the farmhouse was awoken by a scraping sound so shrill as to be almost a shriek, followed by a thunderous thud. The next morning, when the farmer ventured out, he saw the huge stone lying not over the stream but in the middle of the farmyard. Not to be thwarted, he sent John to borrow the four horses again, and the stone was replaced over the stream. John obeyed his master's orders but he allowed himself the comment, 'Won't do no good.'

John was right. The same events occurred the next night, and the night after that. The farmer was a stubborn man but even he could see that he must admit defeat. He called John. 'You had better borrow the horses again. I think we need to return the stone.'

John muttered, 'No need,' and stalked off towards the stable. The farmer was unsure of what he meant until he saw John harnessing one horse to the stone. He began to lead the horse out of the farmyard and the stone moved easily behind. The farmer watched, transfixed, as John and the horse made their way at a brisk pace up the hill with no effort at all.

After the stone was replaced it stayed there unmolested. I don't know whether John said 'I told you so,' but if he did, who could blame him?

ⓧ

There are other little legends about the stones that are hardly stories at all.

The King Stone and The Whispering Knights are said to uproot themselves from their accustomed places each night at midnight and make their way down the hill to Little Rollright Spinney, where they drink from a spring.

The witch who, at the start of this chapter, thwarted the king and then turned herself into an elder tree, is believed by some to still be there, still as a tree. There used to be gatherings at The King Stone at midnight on Midsummer's Eve; the tree would be cut and it would bleed red blood and the king would move his head. It's not clear which elder tree it is; there is more than one. And elder trees only live for sixty years or so; it probably wouldn't be the same one that the witch turned herself into.

Long Compton was noted for its numerous witches. It was said that there were enough of them to pull a load of hay up Long Compton Hill; one might wonder if, being witches, they would have had a need to actually pull it – couldn't they use magic?

A LONG COMPTON MURDER

The belief in witches in Warwickshire continued in the minds of some for an astonishingly long time.

On 15 September 1875, a local man, James Hayward, was returning home in Long Compton from his work on a farm. He had spent the day working on the harvest, but each time he lifted a sheaf with his pitchfork it fell down again and he became convinced that he was a victim of witchcraft. He met 79-year-old Ann (Nanny) Tennant on the road and attacked her. His weapon was the fork that he carried with him.

The report in the *Stratford upon Avon Herald* of 24 September 1875 read:

> On the night in question, between seven and eight o'clock, the poor old woman left her cottage for the purpose of going to a small shop in the village for a loaf of bread. On her return she met Hayward who

had just left his work in the harvest fields and who, without a word on either side, attacked Mrs Tennant with a fork which he was carrying, inflicting such injuries upon her head and body that she died within the course of three hours. In fact, had it not been for the assistance of John Taylor, a farmer, who resided near where the attack took place, he would have killed her on the spot. The only reason that can be assigned for the murder is that Hayward, for some time past, had been under the impression that he was influenced by witchcraft and that Mrs Tennant and several other women in Long Compton were witches, and he was determined to rid the village from them.

At his trial, Hayward seemed confused. A doctor from Hatton Asylum gave his opinion that the defendant, although 'of sufficiently sound mind to understand the proceedings in court' was a 'feeble-minded man thoroughly imbued with the idea of witchcraft'. The doctor assigned to the gaol, however, stated that Hayward 'would not consider an action wrong in the same light as a sane person'.

Hayward himself stated in court that Ann Tennant had bewitched him and stopped him from properly completing his work. There were also, he said, sixteen others in the village who deserved the same as he had done to Ann Tennant. He said that water that was given him to drink as he worked contained witches, and witches had caused cattle and horses in the village to fall sick and even to die. Hayward, in all seriousness, asked the court to weigh the victim's body against a Bible, an old test for witchcraft since no witch can outweigh a Bible.

A reporter wrote at the time of the trial in the *Warwickshire Advertiser*:

> From statements made at the inquest, it seems that these absurd beliefs are shared by others in these parts.

The jury remained in their box to consult with one another for only a few moments before returning a verdict of not guilty on the grounds of insanity. Hayward was detained in Broadmoor Criminal Lunatic Asylum and died there in 1890. Perhaps, though, it was not simply insanity that drove Hayward to commit such a terrible act. Baron Bramwell, the presiding judge, expressed the hope that something could be done 'to disabuse the minds of the people of the village of a belief in witchcraft. It is a most mournful and melancholy state of ignorance.'

Even more remarkable is a statement, made and recorded as recently as 1928 by the son of an eyewitness to the events of 1875. He relates that all the work done by Hayward that day was undone immediately, and that Hayward stabbed Nanny Tennant because she bewitched him. The contributor goes on to relate his own recollections of witchcraft, which he appears to believe, such as an old woman named Faulkner who turned herself into a hare and was shot so that when she returned to human form she could not sit down for weeks; and a man with a team of horses who was advised always to carry a steel needle with him, which would protect him from the effects of witchcraft.

Locally it was observed, well into the twentieth century, that 'the influence of witches goes and comes like the full moon'.

GHOSTS

ONE-HANDED BOUGHTON

In the sixteenth century, a man named Boughton lived in Lawford Hall a few miles north-west of Rugby. He was a strong and vigorous man and a colourful character, well suited to leadership, and when in 1585 Queen Elizabeth's forces clashed with the Spanish in the Netherlands, Boughton was glad to go and fight for the honour of his queen and to support the resistance to Spanish rule.

At Zutphen, Boughton rode into battle with his usual panache. He drew his sword and held it aloft in his right hand to give the men he led a beacon of sorts to follow. Follow him they did, with the sword flashing and glinting in the sun, but the very thing that singled Boughton out and made him easy to follow also made him an easy target. A Spanish musketeer saw the raised arm, the polished blade, and took aim.

Boughton was shot through the wrist, and sword and hand alike fell to the ground.

He was, of course, invalided out of the army and he returned to England and home. He carried on with his life as best he could but he was not a patient man nor a philosophical one. When he saw his friends going hunting as he used to do, it reminded him that he could no longer draw a bow. When he tried to dress and found himself fumbling hopelessly with laces and buttons, he felt humiliated. When his servants brought him a fine meal and he had to be helped to cut up the meat, it was too much and he could have wept with rage and frustration. He was unable, it seemed, to be thankful that he was alive and appreciate what he still had.

As time passed, Boughton's anger and frustration increased. He started to abuse the servants, at first shouting and ranting when they did the slightest thing to irritate him – his food a little too cold, his shirt buttoned too slowly, his horse being brought from the stable a few seconds later than he liked. Before long, the shouting gave way to physical abuse and he would lash out with his one good hand or with either boot.

One by one, the servants began to seek other employment. Some went to serve at other houses, some to work on the land, some simply wandered away to see what life had to offer. When other servants were found to replace them, they too quite soon decided to move on, and so Boughton found himself alone.

Lawford Hall seemed to him, now he was completely alone, to be very large and very lonely. He took to riding or walking along the local lanes, perhaps hoping to see other people, yet if he did meet anyone he was known for being surly and rude.

Years passed in this way. In the local village, Boughton became known as 'One-handed Boughton', a nickname that was perhaps more literal than affectionate. The locals had long since abandoned any attempts to be friendly.

One day, when two of the men from the village were talking, their conversation turned to One-handed Boughton, and it occurred to them that they had not seen him for a little while. How long, they did not know; three days? Four? A week? They disliked the man but they were not cruel and they did not want to think he might have been taken ill with no one to help him, so they went to the priest to ask him what to do.

The priest saw that there was only one thing to be done and that was to find out whether Boughton needed their help. He recruited the two villagers on the spot to accompany him. They weren't keen but, well, an order from the priest must be obeyed. The three of them set out towards Lawford Hall.

No one had come near the hall for many years, and as the three approached, they were shocked at what they saw. The drive was overgrown, the house was dirty and neglected. Seeing that the front entrance was blocked with weeds and clinging ivy, they made their way to the back of the house. The kitchen garden was in a similarly sad state, the walls damp and crumbling, the beds overgrown and choked with weeds, but the kitchen door at least allowed them a way in. They guessed that Boughton had been using this door for some time; certainly he could not have used the front door.

The two villagers hesitated on the threshold; they weren't sure what they might find inside, but they were sure that they wouldn't like it. The priest urged them on, feigning more confidence than he felt.

The three stepped cautiously through the house, keeping close together. Everywhere was damp, musty and dirty, and there were clear signs that One-handed Boughton had for some time been sharing his home with a legion of mice and rats. They entered each room with trepidation, fearing that they would find the

very man they were searching for. The ground floor yielded nothing and the men turned to the stairs, each of them, the priest included, trying not to be the first to the top.

But reach the top they did, and they resumed their search of each room until they came to the last door; the brass handle, being less tarnished than others, suggested habitual use. The three men looked at each other. At last the priest spoke. 'Well if he's anywhere, he's here. We'd better go in. All of us!' He pushed the door open and, closely followed by the two villagers, took a few steps inside.

They were firstly assailed by the smell of a chamber pot clearly in need of emptying, then they took in the contents of the room: a heavy old wardrobe and a chest and a four-poster bed with the curtains closed. The men stared at the bed as if transfixed. There was only one thing to be done. One of the villagers stepped forward and grasping the mouldering curtain, pulled it firmly. It tore from its fixings with a whispering, sighing sound, bringing down a billow of dust and dead insects.

And they had found him. Half propped on pillows, his nightcap askew, his one hand and his stump lying still on the counterpane, his face with the pallor of death was Boughton.

The priest finally broke the silence. 'Ah, you poor soul, I would not have wished it on you to die alone. But you'll terrorise the village no more, will you?'

If only the priest's words had been true.

Lawford Hall, after a time, was renovated and again inhabited by members of the Boughton family. There were repeated attempts to use the room in which One-handed Boughton had died, but no one could ever remain there the night through. Boughton himself, after his death, was repeatedly seen in the area, particularly the lanes around the nearby village of Easenhall. He drives a coach with six horses; quite how he manages six pairs of reins with one hand has never been made clear – but nevertheless there have been many sightings over the years.

In the eighteenth century, the family moved from Lawford Hall to Brownsover Hall and it seems they took ill luck with them; more about that later. But what of Lawford Hall? It was in a poor state of repair, and the man who purchased it wanted it demolished so that he could use the land. Teams of workmen were sent in to systematically dismantle the house. Not all of them stayed. Some had a sense of empty rooms being occupied; some heard footsteps where no footsteps should be; some simply found themselves feeling uncomfortable. One gang of men, the only ones employed at the hall that day, having worked hard at removing roof beams all morning sat together in one of the upstairs rooms to eat their midday meal. The house was draughty and it was halfway through November, so they had wedged one of their long-handled hammers against the door to keep it closed.

As they ate and made quiet conversation, they began to hear, quite clearly, the sound of laboured footsteps on the floor below. Then the footsteps, slow and heavy, began to ascend the stairs.

The foreman turned to the youngest of the workers. 'Go and see who that is, will you, lad?'

The lad turned pale. 'Me? Why me? I – don't know who it is.' The footsteps were now travelling along the landing towards the room.

'Nobody knows who it is,' said the foreman with exaggerated patience. 'That's why I'm telling you to go and look.'

The lad, as slowly as he reasonably could, was placing his meal tin on the floor so that he could do as he had been bidden. But now the footsteps had stopped. Whoever or whatever it was, was outside the door. The handle began to turn. The foreman, all pretence of composure abandoned, said in a wavering voice 'It can't get in, not with the door wedged!' But, inch by inch, the door began to move, the hammer scraping across the bare floorboards and finally rattling to the floor as the door swung fully open.

Afraid to look, but more afraid not to, all the workmen as one man stared into the open doorway. They saw nothing. But the feeling that came over them! A dread chill, like the cold of the grave, descended on each man with a sense of horror and hope-lessness; how long they would have sat there, and what would have become of them will never be known. The foreman, with a huge effort of will, stood up. 'Come on lads, rouse yourselves, get out now!' The others, except for the youngest, stood and made for the door. The foreman grabbed the lad by both arms and dragged him to his feet.

The whole party, keeping close together, hastened along the landing and down the stairs, breaking into a run as they made for the outer door. Once outside the hall, none of them ever set foot in it again.

Nor could anyone else be persuaded to take up the work. Word had spread of the workmen's frightening experience, and perhaps the tale had even grown in the telling. Clearly something must be done, and so twelve clergymen, both Catholic and Protestant, were summoned to the hall. They were led by Parson Hall of Great Harborough, or Harborough Magna, a mile or so east of Easenhall.

It was on Saint Nicholas' Day, 6 December, that the twelve assembled at Lawford Hall; the light was already beginning to fade. Each man carried a candle and a bible. The priest from Great Harborough carried the same and he also had a bottle with a silver stopper. At the foot of the stairs, he lighted his own candle and then the other eleven and the party moved up the stairs and then along the landing to the haunted room. Each of them could feel the temperature dropping and a terrible feeling of oppressiveness growing as they neared and finally entered the former bedchamber.

Once inside, they closed the door and stood in a square, three men to a side and with the unstoppered bottle on the floor in the centre. Parson Hall began to recite the prayers of exorcism, and the others joined him. The sound of footsteps, just as the workers had witnessed, resounded through the house, approaching ever nearer until they stopped outside the door. Every face turned towards the door as it started gradually to open. Every man felt the dread chill seeping into the room, but each continued his prayers. The candles started to go out abruptly one by one as if, rather than being blown by a draught, they were being snuffed. Three candles out. Six candles. Nine candles out. Then the tenth, and the eleventh – only one candle left burning, and that was held by Parson Hall. The flame wavered but kept alight as the clerics recited their prayers and at length the twelve clergymen felt a sense of peace fill the room, and the air became noticeably warmer. Parson Hall stepped forwards and jammed the stopper into the bottle.

Relighting their candles, the twelve men in a procession left the room and the house. Outside in the courtyard, Parson Hall took a lantern and lit it, now leading the others away from the hall and along the road to where there was an old clay pit with a deep lake in its centre. The parson held the lantern high to cast light on the surface of the water, then flung the bottle towards the lake's centre.

∽

But what of the Boughtons of Brownsover Hall? The story goes that Sir Theodosius Boughton was murdered by his brother-in-law, a Captain Donelan, supposedly in a fit of rage in 1780. But Captain Donelan was tried and found guilty of murder the next year, the modus operandi being the administration of laurel water; this sounds rather more like premeditation than a fit of rage. Captain Donelan was executed; some believe that Theodosius Boughton remained at the hall and is there still.

Since that awful event, Brownsover Hall, like Lawford Hall before it, has been haunted by phantom footsteps. Perhaps they run in the family. Disembodied voices have been heard, and cold chills felt. The ghost of a man in eighteenth-century dress is said to haunt the hall. It is now a Grade II listed building and a hotel, and one man staying there reported waking in the night to experience a wave of chill air passing across the surface of the bed. When he reported this to a member of staff in the morning, she knew without being told which room he had been staying in.

Finally, to return to the sightings of a ghostly Boughton driving a coach and six horses in the lanes around Easenhall: this is due, apparently, to negotiations that took place before the spirit was finally enclosed in the bottle. The agreement was that Boughton, or his shade at least, would allow itself to be caught on the condition that it would be released for two hours every night to roam as it pleased. One can only speculate as to the nature of the discussions that may have taken place between Boughton's spirit and the twelve clergymen on that solemn occasion. He must be a rather principled ghost, to keep to his word and return himself to his watery captivity each night.

THE MISERLY WIDOW

The couple, with their 10-year-old daughter, had need of somewhere to live. Their tenancy on their previous home had ended and although sometimes a man and wife can find temporary lodging, it's not so easy for a family with a child. They were delighted, and indeed could hardly believe their luck, when a house in the village became available. They were equally pleased that the house shared a wall with its neighbour. The husband's work took him away for several days at a time and, when the wife and child were there without him, if there should be an emergency they could perhaps bang on the wall to summon help.

The little family moved in during April 1851. The house had been occupied by its owner only a month before, and she had left her furniture, a fact welcomed by the couple since they had none of their own. On their arrival, they were greeted in a friendly enough manner by their next-door neighbour, who nevertheless seemed a little troubled and was at pains to say that if they 'heard anything' in the night, they should call her.

ೞ

Mrs Webb was noted for two things; she was unusually tall and, despite being the widow of a well-off man, unusually mean. She had married relatively late in life, so perhaps she had been used to a life of exceptional economy and found herself unable to change even when life could have become easier.

The inheritor of all her husband's property, she owned the house she lived in and so had no need to pay rent; and she now had plenty of money, more than enough indeed to last her for the rest of her life. But she could be seen in the lanes and woodland near her house, searching for food that she didn't have to pay for: blackberries in the autumn, mushrooms, tiny hedge strawberries, wild garlic leaves, jack-by-the-hedge, hazelnuts, sorrel and even dandelions. Nothing wrong with that, you might think, and she would use the plants she found to supplement the food she reluctantly had to pay for. She would go to the baker and ask for a loaf left over from the day before or the day before that, the older the better because it was cheaper. Sometimes, when she was feeling particularly extravagant or particularly hungry, she would visit a nearby farm and buy a small piece of cheese or an egg.

As time passed, her frugality and self-denial took its toll. As she aged, she grew ever weaker. Her concerned neighbour tried to

look after the old lady, but she refused any help. Eventually, the neighbour sent word to her only relative, her nephew. He lost no time in coming to Mrs Webb's aid but it was too late and all he could do was to comfort her in her last hours.

Mrs Webb's nephew inherited all her worldly possessions, which, it seemed, amounted to little more than her house. He had a house of his own, so he offered his aunt's house for rent with all its furniture and it was not long before the young couple with their daughter moved in.

❧

The little family had been living in their new home for a week. It was a particularly dark night and the young couple were sleeping in the upstairs room at the front of the house when they were awoken by the sound of their bedroom door creaking open. They both sat up in bed, and the wife fumbled with matches, eventually managing to light the bedside candle. There, in the doorway, was a small, white figure. It was their daughter in her nightgown, rubbing her eyes.

'Mummy? Daddy? I think the lady wanted me to come in here.'

The husband sprang out of bed and ran into his daughter's bedroom. No one was there and nothing seemed amiss, so he returned to hear his daughter telling her mother what had happened. She had been asleep in bed, she said, when she woke to see a tall lady standing looking down at her. The lady was beckoning to her and, the little girl said, the lady looked so sad and worried that she got up and followed her. The lady led the way to her parents' bedroom and then passed through the door. The child followed her and, now, she was wondering where the lady had gone.

The parents tried to reassure their daughter that she had just been dreaming, but it seemed the child was in no need of reassurance; she was quite composed and calm.

'But I wonder what the lady wanted,' she said. 'I think she was going to show me something, then she was gone.'

The next night the little girl asked her mother for a slice of bread and a cup of milk to take to bed because the tall lady looked so thin and hungry. The mother indulged her daughter, thinking it would help her to sleep. But later the child again appeared in her parents' doorway, this time asking where Mrs Webb had gone. When asked, she didn't know how she knew the old lady's name; she just kept insisting that the lady wanted to show her something.

The young husband had to travel to a nearby town on business the next day, and because he would be working late, he would have to stay away overnight. He was a little concerned, but his wife assured him she was more than capable of looking after their daughter.

That night, though, it was not the little girl who was disturbed. Her mother went to bed at the usual time and slept peacefully for several hours until she was awoken by a gentle tapping sound. Thinking it was again her daughter, she lit the candle and looked towards the door – but it was closed and no one was there. The tapping continued. The woman listened for a few moments. The sound, more insistent now, seemed to be coming from a cupboard set into the wall on the far side of the room. She drew up her knees under the blankets and wrapped an arm round them, staring intently at the cupboard. The tapping grew louder, now it was a banging like someone thumping a fist on the cupboard over and over. How long she sat there, staring wide-eyed across the room, scarcely breathing, she could not tell.

It was another sudden sound that made her spring from the bed and run from the room. A frantic knocking came from downstairs, from the front door. The woman dashed for her daughter's room, flung the door open and looked in on the child. She was sleeping peacefully, serene and undisturbed. A voice came from outside.

'Are you all right? It's me, from next door. I heard something through the wall!' and the urgent knocking on the front door resumed.

The young mother ran downstairs and wrenched the door open. The neighbour stepped in and enfolded her in a quick hug before, face resolute, she led the way upstairs.

Both women glanced at the child as they passed her open door; she was still sleeping, quite undisturbed. On the threshold of the front bedroom they hesitated. The banging sound was as insistent as ever. The two women each found the other's hand and gripped it tightly, and together they stepped into the room.

The neighbour faced the cupboard and lifted her chin. She spoke with a confidence she did not feel. 'Who's there? Who is it? Is that you, Mrs Webb?' The banging stopped abruptly.

The young mother snatched up the candlestick and by its light the two women approached the cupboard, step by tiny hesitant step. 'Mrs Webb?' the neighbour asked again. The silence seemed only to deepen. She reached out and grasped the handle. Long moments passed, then at last – what else was there to do – she opened the door.

Both of them stared at what was inside. Nothing. It was quite empty, lined with wooden panelling and nothing more. They breathed out as one, unaware until that moment that they had been holding their breath.

Then they heard a sound behind them.

ဢဢ

Earlier that evening, the husband, his business in the town concluded, began to look for a reasonably priced inn where he could stay the night. The first place he tried was too expensive, as was the second. The third had no rooms free and nor did the fourth. When he was turned away from the next three on various pretexts that sounded increasingly like excuses, he began to wonder what was wrong. He wasn't normally superstitious, but he found himself thinking that he wasn't meant to stay in the town, that someone unseen was trying to tell him something. When he thought about his wife and child alone in the house he was gripped with panic without knowing why. He set out for home, resolving to walk all the way if he had to.

He was lucky enough to be taken part of the way by a carter making his way back home after a late delivery in the town. The horse's pace was maddeningly unhurried, but the young man could see that even at a stroll, a long-legged horse covered the ground more quickly than a man would, so he tried to contain his impatience. When about half the distance to the husband's home had been covered, the carter reined in the horse; he had reached the farm he called home. The young man slid down from his seat on the cart, hastily mumbling his thanks, and hurried along the road, still not understanding why he felt such urgency.

Finally reaching his home, he saw that a light flickered and glimmered in the downstairs room. Letting himself in with shaking hands, he was met by three surprised faces looking up at him. His wife, his daughter and the neighbour were all seated on the settle by the fire.

'I just felt I had to come home,' he said. 'But why aren't you all in bed? Has something happened?'

The two women told their story: the banging sound that had frightened the mother and alerted the neighbour; the appeal to Mrs Webb that resulted in silence; looking in the cupboard only to find it empty; nearly jumping out of their skins when they heard a sound behind them.

'It was me!' said the little girl. 'Mrs Webb wanted to show us something and I came to tell mummy. It was in the cupboard, you just couldn't see it.'

The girl told the women that the cupboard had a false back; when they examined it, it proved quite easy to prise away. Behind it were four strong cloth bags, tied at the neck. Each bag was heavy, and the three of them had just brought the bags downstairs to open them by the warmth of the fire when the young man had come home. So all four opened the bags together. The contents

chinked, glittered and glinted. There, in the little front room of a humble little house were heaps of coins, gold and silver coins. It was like a dream.

That is almost all of the story. The young couple sent word to Mrs Webb's nephew that treasure had been found in the house and he came to see for himself. He gave the little family a bag of coins to thank them for their honesty; this they shared with their neighbour.

The morning after the nephew's visit, the little girl came down to breakfast apparently deep in thought. She said, 'The old lady said goodbye last night; she said she was going to her new home and I mustn't be sad because one day I'll see her again.' And perhaps she did.

THE WHITE SWAN

Since the 1880s, Edgbaston has been the home of Warwickshire County Cricket Club, but centuries ago it was hardly even a village, with a few scattered homes and farms. It's only a mile from the centre of Birmingham and in the eighteenth century, with the rise of industry, Edgbaston began to see an increase in building. Newly rich factory owners were drawn to the rural tranquillity of the area and some fine large houses built at that time can still be seen, and of course travellers to a city that was growing in importance needed accommodation.

The White Awan Inn, on Harborne Road, Edgbaston, was founded three hundred years ago. It's still there today, still with the same name, and it's a large, rambling building, just two storeys high and close to the road. In common with many old buildings, it has its share of ghosts, and this is their story.

John Wentworth was a successful businessman with a reputation to maintain. He was well known in Birmingham and it was in that city where, out walking by the market one day, his faithful brown spaniel at his side, he happened to see a comely young maiden. He stopped; he stared; he watched her for some time. She, oblivious to his gaze, strolled from one stall to another. She had a basket over her arm but she was yet to make any purchases. While she had a natural grace and an open and attractive countenance, anyone could see by the clothes she wore, clean but very well worn, that she could have little money to spare. Such a young woman would quite naturally have caution in making her purchases, looking to see where she might save a ha'penny here, a farthing there.

As she made her way through the market, she smiled at the stall holders and the other shoppers, and John could not help noticing how her face lit up each time. Before many minutes had passed he began to think how pleasant it would be if she were to smile at him and he fell to wondering how he could engineer a meeting. But, successful as he was as a businessman, he was yet shy and awkward when it came to speaking to strangers, especially women. And so he stood, silently, as the lovely young woman moved further and further along the rows of stalls, further and further away from him. The spaniel, sitting patiently at John's feet, followed his master's gaze, and his tail thumped slowly.

That evening, John berated himself over and over for his foolish shyness. He resolved to return to the market as often as his business duties allowed and he promised himself that the next time he saw the young woman, he would approach her and talk to her.

Several weeks passed before he did indeed see her once more. He was again out walking with his dog, and the young woman was again strolling through the market with her basket over her arm. To his utter mortification, John found that all his good resolutions fled; there he was, just as immobile and tongue-tied as he had been before. All the witty and amusing conversation openers that he had practised at home in front of the mirror now seemed unbearably foolish and trite. He felt himself growing hot.

Then it happened. The brown spaniel sprang up and ran at the woman, jumping up at her and smearing her clean skirt with his dirty paws. John, all rehearsal forgotten, ran over to her. 'My dear! I am so sorry! How can I apologise? Really, he's only being friendly, but, oh! Look at your skirt!'

Without thinking, he gently took her elbow and steered her to a nearby refreshment stall where he bought her a cup of whey and a small curd tart. For her part, the young woman, blushing a little and smiling shyly, was protesting that it was quite all right and it really didn't matter at all. John, blushing more than a little and smiling so broadly that he was telling himself that he must look quite inane, insisted that she must be allowed to recover her composure and led her to a nearby bench where the two of them sat side by side.

The dog eyed the curd tart with a profound intensity, and this at last seemed to break the ice. The young woman laughed and said, 'What a darling dog! He likes food, doesn't he?' And John agreed, and he started to tell her about his dog, then he told her about himself and the young woman told him a little about her life and before they knew it an hour had gone by. As the church clock chimed the hour the young woman leapt to her feet, saying she really had to be going. John caught her hand. 'When can I see you again? Where do you live? I'll send a carriage.' He was astonished at his own boldness but, after a pause, she smiled and nodded. So it began.

Every week from then on John sent a carriage into Birmingham to collect the young woman. It brought her to The White Swan in Edgbaston, which, though it was rapidly becoming a fashionable area, was still much quieter and more secluded than the centre of Birmingham. At the inn, John would always be waiting, with his dog, in a private room. The young woman would join them, all smiles, and she was like a breath of fresh air. The hours they spent at the inn became the best part of life for both of them, and they spent most of their time together in animated conversation, never running out of things to say, never tiring of one another. They would eat and drink together, and when they ran out of food or drink, John would go to find one of the inn servants to order more. As the staff went about their business, they became accustomed to the sound of John's footsteps behind them, followed by a tap on the shoulder – he had such distinctive footsteps, did Mr Wentworth.

We perhaps need not enquire into what else went on in that private room between the two of them. They would have been content if that room could have become the whole world to them – but their lives were not that simple. John's business and his income relied on his social standing, and it would have been an impossible strain on the young woman to try to become a society hostess, nor was that what she would have desired. So their time together at The White Swan was all they had, and in truth it meant a great deal to them both.

One day, everything changed. John was waiting for his love to arrive and feeling the usual tremors of anticipation – no matter how many times he saw her, the thought of seeing her again caused him to feel excited, nervous and even a little bashful. At once, there was a loud knock at the door, a thumping almost, followed immediately, without waiting for a summons, by the entry of the coachman. He was breathless and flushed. 'Oh sir, something terrible has happened – I couldn't help it – a cart came rushing down the street, out of control, my horses jumped to the side, the axle must have jolted on the kerb and the young lady …'

'What? What, man?' John was already pushing past the coachman and hurrying out to the street.

'She was thrown from the coach sir, I think she's hurt …'

At the carriage, John was tenderly lifting the limp body of his love. He carried her into their private room while shouting for the servants to bring water and bandages for the wound on her head. He sat on an armchair, the young woman still in his arms, the dog whining at his feet. Her eyes fluttered open, she looked into his face and smiled and her eyes closed. Two maids arrived in a fluster, one bearing a bowl of water and the other carrying a linen cloth, but they faltered at the threshold. They could see they were too late.

The servants tactfully withdrew, leaving John with his love cradled in his arms. After a long time – who can say how long?

– he rose with her and laid her gently on the couch. He went to his bag and pulled out a pistol. His face grave, he loaded it and lifted the muzzle to his own head when his eye fell on the spaniel. How could he leave the dog? It was devoted to him and would be bereft without him.

Along the passageway outside the room, two of the servants and the landlord were having a whispered conversation. Yes, it was right to allow him the dignity of a little time alone with the young lady, but after all, this was an inn and a public house and there was a dead body in that room. Wasn't it time that they called someone? A doctor? The constable? The undertaker? Someone should be called and the body should be removed.

Just then they heard the sharp crack of a shot, followed by another. All three ran and burst into the room. They stopped short at the sight before them. Not one body, but three. The young woman, John and the dog.

That was long ago. Today, at the White Swan Inn, people sometimes report hearing distinctive footsteps when there is no one there – no one visible, at least. People sometimes feel a tap on the shoulder, and when they turn round, again, no one. Well, John and the young woman and the dog would have been content if that room could have become the whole world to them, and it seems that perhaps it has. Only sometimes John has to pop out for more food and drink. After all, even ghosts have got to live.

THE GHOSTLY HUNT

There are many tales of the Wild Hunt from all across Britain and beyond. The stories usually involve the devil, or one who is in his thrall, as the huntsman, and the hounds are red-eyed hell-hounds. There is often some act (perhaps speaking to the huntsman, or crossing his path) which you must avoid, or you will be condemned to run with the hounds until the crack of doom. This story is a little different. The devil has kept out of it. But nevertheless, if you should be roaming a certain range of hills at night and you see a pack of hounds followed by a man on horseback, you must take great care not to do the wrong thing. You are sure to regret it.

ℂℵ

Warwickshire is not generally known for its hills, but if you start in the lovely town of Shipston-on-Stour and travel only 3 or 4

miles to the north-west, you will find yourself at the southern
end of a range of hills renowned for their rugged beauty and for
the impressive views they afford. There are some vantage points
from which you can see parts of Worcestershire, Oxfordshire,
Gloucestershire and, of course, Warwickshire.

Nestled among these hills is the ancient village of Ilmington.
Long ago, a man lived here alone, or at least with no other human
sharing his home. For this man loved hunting, and he loved
hunting so much that he kept his own pack of hounds. He had
built kennels with a small run for the dogs behind his house, next
to the stable where he kept his horse. Every day, or every day that
he could, he rode out across the hills with his hounds, urging them
on with wild cries, hunting down any wild animal to cross his path.

One day, he was called away from home to deal with an
unavoidable business matter. He resolved to conclude the transaction as swiftly as he could to allow him to return home in
time to take his hounds out on the hills, if only for a short ride.
He liked the dogs to be hungry when he hunted; he believed it
made them all the keener, so he did not feed them before he set
out that morning.

Perhaps he travelled 4 miles to the south-east to
Shipston-on-Stour. Perhaps he rode 8 miles to the north to
Stratford-upon-Avon. Truth be told, we don't know where he
went to conclude his business; what we do know is that he was
unexpectedly delayed, the matter taking far longer than the time
he had allowed. As he was setting out for home, the sun had just
set, and while there was still plenty of light left in the sky, it would
very soon be fading to darkness. It would have been judicious to
find somewhere to stay for the night, but there was no one else to
look after the hunting hounds, and besides, he still had foolish
hopes of going hunting that day.

It was completely dark when he reached home. As he approached, he could hear the hounds making an unearthly row: howling, baying, wailing. They had been left all day with no food or exercise, no hunting or prey, and by the sound of it they had worked themselves up to a near-frenzy. The man dismounted his horse and hurried to the kennels to see what was the matter. At the back of the house it was, if anything, even darker, and he had almost to feel his way to the kennel gate. Once he found it, he fumbled to find the lock and to fit the key into it. The delay, or perhaps the uncertainty, drove the hounds into an even wilder state. Finally, the gate was unlocked and the man flung it wide open. He had only a very few moments to regret his actions; his own hounds leapt upon him, snarling and biting, ripping and tearing until there was little of him left.

Or rather, there was little of his corporeal form left. The next night, at the exact time of his death, he reappeared. As if nothing had happened, he released his hounds, mounted his horse and rode out to the hills. Here he rode, hunting for hours until the first glimmer of dawn; then he vanished.

It was so long ago, they must all be ghosts now: rider, horse and hounds. Sometimes they are only heard; sometimes they have been seen. One thing is sure. If you happen to get caught out on the hills after dark and you should have the luck (good or bad according to your point of view) to see the ghostly hunt, you must not look into the huntsman's eyes. If you do, he will have you in his power forever. What might he do with you? No one knows for no one has lived to tell the tale.

THE FOXCOTE FEUD

This story, like the one above, takes place in the environs of Ilmington. Foxcote House, a large eighteenth-century country house, has been a Grade II listed building since 1952 and is just a mile and a half from the village. It's privately owned, as it was at the time of this story.

Many years ago, a Mr Canning was the owner of the Foxcote estate. There was a neighbouring estate owned by a Captain Barnsley; perhaps it would be reasonable to assume that, as both men owned estates in this hilly area of Warwickshire, they might have a lot in common. They each had similar patches of woodland to manage; they both had herds of cattle and sheep roaming the estate; they both like to hunt the game that lived wild on their estates. They surely could have discussed their experiences and their successes and failures to their mutual benefit. But they didn't.

It was hard to say when it started. To begin with, when Mr Canning and Captain Barnsley happened to meet on the road, they might exchange a nod and pass on. From time to time, they might pause on their way and exchange a few words, each man taking the opportunity to extol the virtues of his fine livestock, or to remark on the quality of the timber yielded by his woodland – and so on. Occasionally, they would be travelling on foot; sometimes they passed one another by on horseback; but one day, it all changed.

Captain Barnsley had always been a bit of a dandy, in contrast to Mr Canning. He favoured lace cuffs, where Canning wore plain linen; Barnsley enjoyed wearing velvet, while Canning stuck to serviceable thornproof tweed; Barnsley's favourite horse was a spirited, fine-boned thoroughbred, while if Canning had business in the town, he rode a heavy, placid farm horse. Then, one afternoon, riding home from a visit to Stratford, Canning saw something bowling along the road towards him which, even by Barnsley's standards of ostentation, was excessive. It was a very fine, highly polished carriage drawn by six matched horses, and undoubtedly it looked impressive, but it was hardly suited to the narrow roads and lanes of this rural location. People who lived in that area, and many like it, found a farm cart or a pony and trap quite sufficient. But here it was, a coach and six, and out of the window leaned Captain Barnsley.

He called to the coachman to halt, and he hailed Canning. 'Marvellous hunting this morning! I've so many pheasants and hares, I'm off now to give them away to friends.'

Canning reined in his horse. Barnsley had ducked back inside the carriage and was rummaging around on the floor. After a moment or two, he popped his head out of the window again, a hare and a pheasant in hand. 'Here,' he said, 'take these. I know you don't have much game on your land.' He grinned.

'No, thank you,' said Canning stiffly. 'I have plenty of my own.'

'Won't you change your mind? I'm sure your game can't compare to mine!' And, without listening to Canning's answer, Barnsley called to the coachman to drive on. His parting shot, as the carriage pulled away, was, 'Do feel free to hunt on my land. You really will find the sport is far superior!'

Canning was left to seethe at the implied slight.

From that day on, things went from bad to worse between the two men. Barnsley seemed to have got the devil in him and, every time he saw Canning, contrived to mention how superior was the game on his land. Canning, for his part, was quite unable to rise above the taunting or laugh it off, and couldn't stop himself from throwing a boast or a rebuff back at Barnsley, and so the relationship between the two men deteriorated day by day.

At last the crisis came. It just so happened that on this particular day, both men were on foot. Canning was walking back from Ilmington; Barnsley was walking towards it. It had been a frustrating morning for Canning; the sale of beef he had been planning for had not come to fruition, and he was feeling discouraged and thwarted. The last person he wanted to see at that moment was Captain Barnsley, but there he was: merrily whistling as he strode along, brimming with exuberance.

Captain Barnsley raised a hand to hail Canning and said, 'How are you today? And how's the hunting coming along? I've bagged the most superb birds this week. Such a shame …' and no one will ever know how that sentence was going to end, for Mr Canning, with a kind of strangled shriek, had raised his heavy walking stick and brought it down hard on Captain Barnsley's head. The man, without a stagger or a cry, hit the ground with a sudden thud, his face pressed into the hard stones of the road while thick dark blood spread around him.

Canning, rigid with shock at what he had done, stared down at his rival's body. It was so still, such a terrible contrast to the man as he had been only moments before. Canning roused himself and stared wildly around – all was quiet, nobody had seen. He began to run, still grasping the bloodied walking stick, and ran until he reached home. There, he rushed up to his chambers and stuffed a travelling bag with some clothes and as much money as he had to hand. Then he hurried down to the stables where, watched by an astonished stable lad, he saddled his horse, mounted and cantered away.

He rode to the Stratford to Banbury turnpike, where he waited for a coach that would take him south. His horse he let loose to amble back home; Canning himself never went home again. From Banbury he continued on to London and from there to the coast. He sailed to France, and there he vanished; no word has ever been heard of where he went or what he did.

Captain Barnsley's body was, of course, discovered and buried with due ceremony. As Canning fled at the time of Barnsley's death and the antipathy between the two men was well known, he was blamed for the murder but never stood trial because, as we have heard, he was never found.

Barnsley, though, seems convinced that Canning is to be found somewhere in the Ilmington hills. He has from time to time been seen in a now-ghostly coach drawn by six horses, ever searching for his murderer. If you should come across the spectral carriage on some dark night, you will know if it is Barnsley's; while the captain remains intact, the coachman and the horses have inexplicably mislaid their heads.

GUY OF WARWICK

Guy's Cliffe, overlooking the River Avon and less than a mile from the centre of Warwick, was for centuries known as a home for hermits. Above the cliff is a ruined house also known as Guy's Cliffe; although the house is now little more than a shell, its chapel is still intact, and in the chapel may be seen a statue, 8ft high and 600 years old. The statue is carved from the living rock face and it is damaged, you might even say mutilated. It shows a knight, possibly wearing armour, a large shield on his left arm and with his right arm missing. It is the oldest image known of Guy of Warwick, but we cannot expect a likeness; it was made 400 years after his death.

GUY'S EARLY YEARS

When Guy was nearly grown to manhood he was honoured to fulfil the role of cup-bearer to Rohaud, his master. Rohaud was accustomed to hosting a festival lasting several days at Pentecost, which, in the year our story begins, was in early summer. At the welcoming feast, Guy was replenishing the drinks of the prominent and influential men who shared Rohaud's top table when Rohaud looked up. 'Guy, no one is serving on the ladies' table. Go and see if there is anything they need.'

Now, in those days, rich and powerful families had strict rules about the behaviour of women. Young women, the daughters of the families, were especially protected and shielded from what was considered unnecessary contact with men. Thus it was that as Guy approached the ladies' table he saw for the first time Rohaud's daughter, Felice, at close

quarters. She was at the centre of a group of young women, her friends and attendants, and they were all laughing at some jest or witticism. Guy was transfixed. Her grace, her vitality, oh, the very aliveness of her: in a moment he had lost his heart.

Unfortunately, it appeared to onlookers that he had lost his senses. After a few moments Felice noticed him. 'What is it, boy?'

Guy forced himself into a state of some self-control and he enquired, in as normal a voice as he could muster, whether the ladies required anything that he might fetch for them. The ladies were perfectly happy, it seemed, and Guy was sent away.

From that moment, Guy began to plan how he might win the heart and the hand of the fair Felice.

∽

One thousand years ago, Rohaud, Earl of Warwick, of Oxford and of Buckingham, was one of the most powerful lords in England. He was revered as a fierce fighter and leader of men, and his riches were legendary. His trusted steward was a loyal and prudent man named Segward. It was deemed an honour when Rohaud took on Segward's son Guy as his cup-bearer, and it was indeed a further honour when Rohaud engaged Heraud of Arden, a renowned knight, to instruct Guy in courtly ways and knightly skills. Guy was quick and strong and he listened well to his mentor, such that soon none at Rohaud's court could compete with him at hawking, hunting and combat. But Guy was not a knight. Guy was the son of a steward.

As the daughter of a rich and powerful man, Felice attracted the attentions of many rather less rich and powerful men who were anxious to forge an advantageous allegiance. She had thus far resisted their attentions, for Felice was a young woman with a mind of her own. Her father had brought masters from Toulouse to instruct her and she had become learned in the seven arts. She was literate, she understood arithmetic, she could both play and write music, she knew geometry, she could speak eloquently, she had knowledge of the stars and she was trained in logic. She was indeed fiercely logical. Her freedom of thought and her eloquence were a formidable combination.

On the night of the Pentecost feast, when the festivities were over, Guy retired to his room and deliberated on what he should do. After a while, he made up his mind. He jumped to his feet and made his way through the sleeping house to find Felice's room. Against all protocol, and at great risk to himself should he be caught, Guy entered her room, where he found Felice still awake, reading by candle light. He fell on his knees, imploring her to be his, for he was dying of love. If she would not accept him, he vowed, he would have to kill himself.

Felice put down her papers and regarded him with undisguised scorn. 'So, what would you have me do? I am the daughter of an earl, you are the son of a steward. Have you any idea how many of this country's noblemen have sought to marry me? Seriously, tell me, what do you envisage?'

Guy mumbled an apology, rushed from her room and stumbled back to his own. He flung himself on his bed and that is where he was found when he did not appear for his duties as usual the next day and a servant was sent to seek him out. Over the next few days, Guy remained in his room and he became more and more pale and ill-looking. The Earl Rohaud was not an unkind man and he had some fondness for the young man; he became quite concerned and he sent for a wise doctor but it was to no avail.

Felice too began to worry about Guy. Really, she hardly knew him but she had always heard good reports of him and she certainly wished him no harm. One night she had a vivid dream. In her dream a wise woman appeared to her and told her that Guy was good-hearted and true and that he would win great honour for her sake. On waking, Felice resolved to see what she could do to help the young man. She went to see him.

On being shown into his room, Felice was taken aback at how pale and weak he looked – this young man who had won admiration for his strength and his skills as a fighter. To see him laid so low was shocking. She smiled gently. 'Guy, what is all this? Why do you do this?'

He looked on her so lovingly, it almost broke her heart. 'I don't know how to live without you,' he said simply.

'Well you must. I can only love one of noble rank.' And, thinking that to prolong the conversation would do him no good, she took her leave of him.

But Guy began to smile. He sat up. He swung his legs out of bed and began to look around for his clothes. Soon he was dressed and making his way along the corridor, keeping one hand on the wall to steady himself, so weak had he become.

He found Rohaud in the hall. The earl smiled in pleasure at seeing the young man up and about again, and he invited Guy to sit with him. Guy came straight to the point. 'I know I am the son of a steward, but Sir Heraud of Arden has trained me, and I believe I can say he is pleased with me. I know as much as anyone of the knightly arts, and many will admit that my skill excels that of most others. Might I then be considered for a knighthood?'

Earl Rohaud knew the value of the young Guy. Like his father, he was honest and loyal and he was well suited to join the earl's company of knights. Without having to give it much thought, Rohaud agreed to Guy's request.

The ceremony took place less than a month later. Guy and several other young men were knighted together, and the drinking and feasting lasted long into the night. Guy, however, was little interested in the merrymaking; instead, he watched and waited the whole evening, alert for the opportunity that finally came. Felice, feeling a little warm, took herself outside to wander in the rose garden. Guy followed her and she turned at his approach.

'Felice! My one and only true love! You said you could only love one of noble rank. Well, now I am a knight. Will you now love me?'

Felice considered her words. 'You may be a knight, but you have been one for only three hours. There is much more to being a knight than being knighted – that was my father's act, not yours. I cannot possibly consider you if you have done no knightly deeds. Where are your vanquished foes? Where are your noble accomplishments? Where your valorous adventures?'

If Guy was downcast, it was not for long. After just a little thought, he said, 'My lady, for your sake and to win your love I will undertake worthy quests and exploits. I will be worthy of you!'

Felice smiled. The memory of that smile stayed with him for a very long time.

The day after the ceremony, Guy went to his father. 'I wish to travel to foreign lands to prove myself as a true knight. May I have your permission to go?'

Segward gave his blessing with mixed feelings. For the son of a steward to embark on a knightly quest was a marvellous thing, but also fraught with danger. His agreement was with conditions. 'You must not go alone. It is the custom for companies of knights to set out on adventures together. Ask Sir Heraud of Arden if he will accompany you. He will be able to advise and guide you. And Sir Thorold and Sir Urry are good men; take them as your companions.'

And thus it was decided.

SIR GUY BEGINS HIS QUEST

Early one midsummer morning, the four companions set out. Pleasant it was indeed to ride southwards through the Kingdom of England as the knights journeyed through great forests, over green hillsides and past villages and farms until at last they sighted the sea and the port of Dover.

Sir Heraud reined in his horse and addressed his companions. 'There it is: the port. There, we will be able to find a ship to take us away from England's shore and into foreign lands. Who knows when or even if we might return?' He turned to Guy. 'Is this still your desire?'

Guy considered his answer. Sir Heraud had always been more than a mentor to him; Guy thought of him as a second father and respected him greatly. When he at last spoke, his answer was simple. 'I have to go.'

So the four knights rode on. They found a ship bound for France easily enough and they sailed the next day. When they disembarked, Heraud took the lead. 'There is a city called Rouen five or six days' ride south of here. I think we should go there and see what news we can gather.'

Rouen was full of activity. Almost every house bore bright streamers and flags, and knights and squires thronged the streets. There was a blacksmith's shop where a queue of bored-looking squires held armfuls of weapons while the blacksmith sharpened the edges of lances, swords and axes. Guy, Heraud, Thorold and Urry made their way through the crowds and eventually found lodgings at an inn; they asked the innkeeper why the city was so busy.

'Oh, it's not usually like this. There's a great tournament, it's in honour of Regnier, the Emperor of Germany. He has travelled here with his daughter. The prizes are a white falcon, a fine horse and a brace of greyhounds. But that's not why so many men are drawn to compete. No, the thing is, whoever is victorious at the close of day, well, he will be allowed to ask for the princess's hand in marriage. The Emperor's daughter! Well, what knight wouldn't want that?'

Guy thought, straight away, that he wouldn't. But he would very much like a chance to have the honour of winning. That would make a fine story to tell at home in Warwick.

The four knights set off the next morning to take part in the tournament. They found themselves among a great crowd; many were knights on horseback with their attendant squires, and many were the citizens of Rouen, most of them on foot, off to see an exciting spectacle. None, though, was more excited than Guy. He was half Heraud's age, and Thorold and Urry were a good ten years his senior. Unlike his companions, this was Guy's first tournament and his first chance to try his skill outside of Warwick. He was wide-eyed with wonder at playing a small part in this momentous occasion, and he found himself trembling with anticipation.

The tournament field was vivid with flags, pennants, brightly coloured pavilions and, of course, the thronging crowds. At the far end, on a raised platform and under a richly embroidered canopy, was seated the Emperor Regnier with his daughter at his side. Knights formed into cohorts to take part in mock battles, thrilling re-enactments of warfare that nevertheless caused bloodshed. Many men were carried to the infirmary tent. Guy watched it all with intense fascination – then the single combat began. Men fought on horseback and on foot, and one by one knights lost their battle and had to leave the tournament. Guy's turn came, and, inexperienced as he was, his natural strength, speed and agility allowed him to win the bout with ease.

As the day wore on, knight after knight was eliminated from the contest. Of the four companions, Thorold was the first, then Sir Urry and Sir Heraud. At last, as the sun was sinking in the sky, there were two contestants left: Guy and Otho, Duke of Pavia.

Otho was a mature man in his prime, with a confident, even arrogant bearing. As he sat astride his horse, waiting for the signal to begin the joust, he looked at Guy and then pointedly turned to gaze upon the princess – the prize for the victor. The signal came and the two levelled their lances and rode at each other.

On the platform, some 50 yards away, the Emperor Regnier leaned forward and watched with interest. One of these men could be his future son-in-law. What better way to secure a suitably brave and warlike knight to lead the people of the land and to protect its borders than to have the best men fight it out? Now, the horses' hooves thundered and there was an audible clash as the point of Guy's lance struck Otho's breast-plate. The older man was knocked back in the saddle by the force of the impact. He flailed his arms wildly seeking to save himself but in vain and he tumbled to the ground.

The princess sat upright in her gilded chair, her face betraying no emotion. She was acquainted with one of these men and she would wish anything but to be his wife. Was the other, the younger one, preferable? She had no way of telling. As she watched Guy dismount to continue the combat on foot, as the rules of knightly conduct dictated, the princess mused that the lowliest kitchen maid in the palace had more freedom in choosing a man to spend her life with than did the emperor's daughter. She watched as Guy offered his hand to Otho to help him to his feet. It did not surprise Regnier to see Otho knock away the proffered hand in what could be nothing but childish pique.

Otho heaved himself to his feet and drew his sword and the battle recommenced. The princess contrived to appear to be watching while allowing her gaze to slip towards the distant horizon. She had no desire to witness any more bloodshed this day. But she could not stop herself from hearing the relentless clash and clash and clash of steel on steel and the gasps from the watching crowd. Until there was silence. The young woman held her gaze for a moment and then dared to look. Otho was lying on his back. His sword – it must have been wrested from him – lay some feet away. The young knight stood over him, the point of his sword at Otho's throat. The contest had found its victor.

A little later, Guy was presented to the Emperor, who signalled to his servants to bring forward a fine horse, a hawk and a brace of hunting dogs. 'And there is of course one further prize,' he said, gesturing towards his daughter.

Guy flushed. He was as awkward, hesitant and faltering as the princess was impassive. 'I am deeply conscious of the honour, my lord, and the lady – well the lady can hardly be surpassed by any. Not any in this land, at least. But I am betrothed to another and to her I must be faithful, as my calling dictates.' He bowed low, and thus avoided seeing the impotent anger in the Emperor's face.

As Guy later made his way back to his companions, a man stepped into his path. It was the Duke of Pavia, Otho. He glared at Guy. 'I will remember this day and I will remember you until the time comes when I will have my revenge. Make no mistake. My memory is long and I will see the slight I have suffered today vindicated.' He turned on his heel and walked away, giving Guy no chance to reply.

THE QUEST CONTINUES

Following the tournament, Guy contrived to have his prizes, the horse, hawk and hounds, sent back to Warwick as proof of his success. But fearing that he had not done enough to secure Felice's hand in marriage – he had after all not given the Emperor the complete truth when he claimed he was betrothed – Guy and his companions continued on their travels.

Over the course of a year the comrades journeyed together, seeking out tournaments, where they acquitted themselves well, and fighting in battles and wars on the side of justice. When the year was done, Guy felt such a longing for home and for Felice that he resolved to return to England to give an account of himself.

When the four comrades arrived home in Warwick, the whole of Earl Rohaud's court turned out to welcome them. Segward was delighted, having feared that he may never see his son again, and the Earl himself greeted Guy with a sincere warmth. Both of the older men marvelled at how much Guy seemed to have matured in his time abroad.

With the celebratory feasting lasting three days, and with everyone wanting to hear the stories of the four knights' adventures over and over again, it was some time before Guy could contrive to speak to Felice in private. As he had done over a year before, he followed her out to the rose garden where she loved to walk. Typically, he spoke without guile. 'Felice, I have told you of my love for you and you know I wish to be your husband. I have journeyed to foreign lands in search of adventure and tests of my courage. Have I now done enough? Will you accept me as your suitor?'

Felice said, 'No.'

She let her gaze rest on a full-petalled red rose, and she traced the edge of the bloom with her forefinger. 'I do not deny that you have done well. But you have not done enough. What would you do? Have a year of adventuring and then return to a life of idleness? Then you would be no better than any other knight. I do not want a man who is as mediocre as the rest. I want a man who is the best.' She turned and walked away.

Segward the steward was deeply concerned when he heard of his son's intention to go travelling once more, and Earl Rohaud also expressed his disquiet. Guy was adamant that he must go, and no matter how pressed, he would not reveal his reasons for wanting to leave again so soon after his return.

Once again, his faithful travelling companions agreed to go with him and it was not long before Sir Guy, Sir Heraud, Sir Thorold and Sir Urry rode out once more together. Would their leave-taking have been so blithe if they could have known what was to befall them?

❦

This time, on landing in France, the comrades rode east towards northern Italy. The weather was mild and they journeyed for a fortnight pleasantly enough and with little incident. One day, while seeking refreshment in a village, they heard of a tournament in a town near Pavia and so they made their way there and enrolled as contestants. This time, Heraud, Thorold and Urry were each more successful than Guy, who sustained a slight injury. When Guy's wound had been treated, the comrades discussed which direction and which roads they should take next. None of them noticed the insignificant-looking man in a blue tunic who was standing casually nearby and who, once they had decided on their destination, hurried to mount his horse and rode away at speed.

Later that day, the four knights found themselves approaching a great forest. They were aware of the dangers of leaving open country and of losing their ability to see any ruffians who might be approaching them, but the forest looked so vast that it seemed to be a choice of taking the track that ran through it or of retracing their steps.

☙❦

A man in a blue tunic galloped up to the Duke of Pavia's palace, halted his horse and hurried up the steps. The guard knew to expect him and allowed him in to speak to the Duke. After a brief conversation, Duke Otho called a servant to fetch payment for the man; another servant was sent to muster the best of the Duke's knights.

The Duke gave the fifteen knights clear instructions: 'Kill the three older ones; Guy must be taken alive. Bring him to me and you will be well rewarded. I have a place waiting in my dungeon for young Sir Guy. Once I have him, he will never leave.'

☙❦

The four companions rode for an hour or more along a well-used track without seeing another soul. There was space enough for two to ride side by side, and Guy and Heraud took the lead, with Thorold and Urry behind them. The canopy of trees cast a cool shade that felt pleasant and restful but it sometimes made it difficult to see very far ahead.

The path curved to the left and out of sight. Suddenly four knights appeared. Their swords were drawn and it was clear that they were preparing to attack. Heraud leaned towards Guy and whispered urgently, 'Turn and ride back the way we have come. There is no shame in retreat when you are wounded. The three of us can deal with these men. Go, quickly.'

But Guy would not countenance such a thing. Four against four. It would not be much of a contest. The comrades drew their swords and were about to ride forward and meet the challenge when they heard the rustle of leaves on the path behind them. Four more knights, swords in hand. And then, appearing from between the trees, three or four knights on either side.

The fight was immediate and desperate. In an instant, Guy found himself set upon by three men. Fierce and fast in spite of his wound, Guy, wielding his sword like a battle axe, killed two of them within a few moments; the third retreated a little way along the path, allowing Guy to turn and help his friends. Sir Thorold was desperately trying to hold four assailants at bay – as Guy rode up he saw Thorold strike a death blow to one, who fell from his horse. Guy killed a second while Thorold's flashing sword mortally wounded a third. At that moment the fourth saw his chance and he plunged his sword into Thorold's heart. Thorold died silently. Guy cried loud and long as he fell upon Thorold's killer, striking the man down to the ground.

Sir Urry and Heraud, their horses side by side, were holding off six or seven attackers. The narrowness of the path was at least to the friends' advantage; the Duke's men could not all attack at once. Guy, grief fuelling his fury, hacked wildly at

the two nearest assailants. One, suffering a blow to his side, reeled from his horse, fell and lay still. The second, his neck hacked almost through by Guy's savagely swinging sword, dropped like a stone.

Heraud was furthest from Guy. He was now fighting with two men, grimly parrying their every cut and thrust, barely holding them off. Two knights had also fallen upon Sir Urry. His blood was staining his garments, yet still he fought with a frantic urgency. Guy urged his horse over to one of the men and brought his sword down on his head, cleaving it open. As he did so the second man stabbed Urry's chest. Urry turned to look at Guy, his mouth opened wordlessly and he fell.

Heraud, seeing Sir Urry slain, turned with a wild yell from his own combat, hewing at Urry's killer until he, too, fell. But Heraud's attackers saw their chance. One struck Heraud's head with a terrible blow, and Guy saw his beloved mentor fall to the ground.

Sword raised, Guy rode towards the two men, but they had seen enough of the young knight's ferocity in battle. They turned their horses' heads away and fled with all speed.

Guy lost the will to fight any longer. He let the men get away. He dismounted his horse and went to each of his friends in turn. Long he looked on each man. He gently straightened disarrayed limbs, he tenderly moved their heads into a comfortable position, he closed their eyes, he said a prayer over each of them.

How long he stood in silent prayer he could not say. The heaviness of his heart, the feeling of impotent outrage, the grief that was beginning to cast its pall over him, were near to unbearable. He mounted his horse and rode away, seeking help.

After a time he came to a forest glade where a little stream chuckled and sparkled in the dappled sunlight. On the bank of the stream was a small hut with a thin trail of grey-blue smoke rising from a hole in the centre of the roof. Guy called out and a man appeared in the doorway. Guy said, simply, 'Help me.'

The man, a hermit, seeing that Guy was bloodied and wounded, hurried forward to help him down from his horse but Guy refused to dismount. He told the man that he had friends who were more in need of help, and so the hermit walked alongside as Guy rode back along the path.

At the scene of the attack, Guy dismounted and showed the hermit the bodies of his friends. Together, they lifted and laid the knights over their horses' backs. 'And these others?' asked the hermit, gesturing towards Duke Otho's fallen men.

'A few of their company escaped,' said Guy shortly. 'I expect they will return for the bodies.'

The hermit and Guy led the sad procession back to the glade. 'Will you bury them?' asked Guy.

The hermit said, 'This glade is a peaceful place. It has a holiness of its own. I can bury your friends here if you wish.'

Guy nodded. 'I am grateful. These men were my friends and close companions. And yet,' he went to Heraud's horse and laid his hand gently on the limp body of his mentor and oldest friend. 'I somehow cannot bear to be parted from this man.'

'If you ride on a few miles,' said the hermit, 'you will come to an abbey. Take your friend there. The abbot is a wise man.'

Guy offered a solemn goodbye to Sir Thorold and Sir Urry in that peaceful glade. He left their horses with the hermit as payment. Mounting his own horse and leading Heraud's horse with its sad burden, he bid the hermit farewell.

It was a strangely pleasant ride; the road left the forest and passed through beautiful green countryside with small birds singing on every side. As Guy approached the abbey, several monks, seeing his approach, ran forward to help him. Heraud was carried inside with Guy walking dolefully behind. The abbot was called, and on seeing Guy, wounded and bloodied as he was, hastened to help him. Guy stepped back. 'I do not need help. Please, Father Abbot, my dearest friend lies here. Can you bury him with care and honour?'

At that, his grief finally overcame him and he hastened from that holy place. Though a great weariness was now close to defeating him, he mounted his horse once more and rode back the way he had come, Heraud's horse following.

In the forest glade Guy found the hermit kneeling in prayer beside two low mounds of fresh earth. Guy all but fell from his horse and the hermit half carried him into the hut. There, Guy stayed while days turned into weeks. The hermit tended his bodily wounds, which, in time, healed; Guy's melancholy humour was not so easily mended.

The day came when Guy, though still carrying a great weight of sadness, felt ready to go on his way. He thanked the hermit as best he could for all he had done, though to his own ears Guy's words sounded sadly inadequate. He rode away, Heraud's horse following behind like a faithful dog.

Guy rode for two days without meeting another soul, when he saw a man in a monk's habit, the hood raised, seated on a rock at the roadside and seemingly in contemplation. Unwilling to break the man's reverie, yet craving gentle human company, Guy reined in his horse and waited quietly. At length, the man glanced up. 'Guy! Is it you?' and the hood fell back to reveal Heraud.

Guy was at first afraid, then incredulous. Heraud told his story. 'I was near to death when you took me to the abbey. The blow to my head had stunned me and, the abbot told me, it was several more days before I came even a little to my senses. The abbot has great skill as a healer and he cared for me himself over many long days and nights. When at last I was well again, I resolved to search for you. They gave me one of the monks' old robes and I swore I would wear it until I found you.'

The two embraced and went on their way side by side, their joyousness at once again being together tempered by their sadness and shock at losing their two dear friends.

MORE ADVENTURES

As Guy and Heraud travelled on, they talked over their plans. Should they seek further adventures or should they return home? Guy mused on how long it had been since he had seen Felice. Heraud suggested that they should sleep on it and talk more in the morning.

That night, they found a wayside hostel and so shared the last of the evening with fellow travellers. The conversation went round, and some people who had recently come from Greece said that the good king of that land was under siege by a Saracen army and was sorely in need of help. Guy took this to be a sign, and the next morning he set out with Heraud on the road to Greece. As the pair travelled from town to town, they gathered a company of knights, a few here and a few there, until the company was sixty strong.

As this bold company drew nearer to Greece and the besieged king, Guy began to have a recurring dream. He was in the forest glade with the hermit, and he was sleeping in the hermit's hut. In his dream he awoke, and he went outside into the light of a full moon. He walked along the track through the silent forest; he felt a strange lightness in his body, such that his feet barely seemed to touch the path. He recognised that he was approaching the turn in the path where he and his friends had been set upon by Duke Otho's men. The way became darker. He noticed a faint smell of corruption, growing stronger with every step, though there were now no corpses. He felt oppressed, as if by a weight bearing down on him, and his feet began to drag on the ground. He knew the forest floor to be dry, yet it became as if he was walking through thick mud. He looked down, and with a jolt saw what it was that sucked at his feet. Blood. The path was deeply mired in thick, cloying blood. He tried to get away, to run back to the moonlit glade, but the blood held his feet like grasping hands. He flailed his arms, vainly reaching for a tree trunk or branch, anything to help free him. And he woke from the dream, always at this point, wild-eyed and breathing hard.

The company reached the town where the king lay under siege. After many battles where many good men fell, and due in no small part to Guy's ability to inspire the troops, the siege was lifted. And Guy continued to dream.

The Greek king was full of gratitude; he offered his daughter Clarice in marriage to Guy. Guy accepted, but when he was shown the ring that had been made for the wedding, he remembered his promises to Felice (how could he have forgotten?) and, with many expressions of regret, he took his leave of the king. At last, Guy and Heraud began to make their slow journey back to England.

THE DUN COW

The friends travelled for weeks through Europe to France, where they found a ship bound for Dover. From there, their journey took them northwards.

While Guy and Heraud were still in France seeking a passage to England, the Abbot of Coventry was having an adventure of his own. He had spent a few days in Daventry on church business, and he was now making his way back to the abbey in Coventry. He had ridden 12 miles or so on his mule, and the animal was becoming weary, with another 7 miles to go. The abbot thought it wise to dismount and seat himself on the grass, his back supported by an oak tree while the mule cropped the grass and rested.

The day was pleasantly warm and the abbot dozed off, slumping comfortably against the accommodating tree trunk. He was startled awake by shouting. He sat upright and saw two men running towards him. They dropped to their knees on the grass before him. 'Help us Father! It's the cow!'

The abbot asked them to explain. The men told him they were fleeing a monstrous, murderous cow. They had been crossing Dunsmore Heath when they saw it – a huge dun-coloured beast with fiery eyes and vast black curving horns.

The abbot was not known for his credulity, but he was a kind man and he told the men they had better show him this astonishing creature, this monstrous Dun Cow.

The abbot mounted his mule and the men, with some trepidation, led him in the direction of the heath. They passed several sheep lying dead in a field; the poor animals looked as though they had been gored. A horse at the side of the road seemed to have been trampled to death, as did an old pedlar. The abbot dismounted and insisted that the men lift the body on to the back of the mule so he could be taken for a decent burial.

Becoming persuaded that the men had been telling the truth, the abbot decided what he must do. He asked the men to accompany him on his walk to Coventry; when the three had arrived, the abbot sent the men with the mule to the abbey to report the abbot's safe return and to request the burial of the pedlar. The abbot himself made his way to the home of the Earl of Mercia.

The earl, seeing that the abbot was dusty and weary from his journey, sent a servant for refreshment. The abbot came straight to the point. He reported to the earl the fantastic story that the two men had told him, and then described the sights he had seen on passing through Dunsmore Heath. 'I have not seen the monster,' he said, 'but it evidently is a mortal threat to the people of Mercia. Will you see to it that this creature is destroyed?'

Knowing that the abbot was not a man to make such a request idly, the earl sent for messengers. He instructed them to travel in all directions throughout Mercia, proclaiming that whichever man destroys the Dunsmore Heath Dun Cow shall be awarded gold rings, an ivory cup and finely wrought chain mail.

☙❧

Guy and Heraud had been riding for nine or ten days when they heard the news. They made haste to see the earl, who met them in the courtyard of his house. He explained the reason for so unusual a quest. 'The people who live on the heath are in terror for their lives and for the safety of their livestock. They stay in their houses as much as they can. This is no ordinary cow; it's more than twice the normal height, it's huge, and it has killed people and animals alike. There are some who think it is not of this world. I should tell you, some are saying that it cannot be killed. This is a perilous task.'

Guy pledged to do his utmost to rid the people of Dunsmore Heath of the savage brute. The earl warned him again of the danger of the mission and was impressed with Guy's quiet resolve and his apparent lack of bravado or arrogance.

Pausing only to gird on his armour and to ask Heraud to wait with the earl, Guy rode out, taking the south-easterly road towards the heath. He had travelled for 7 miles or so when he began to see signs of the creature. Cattle, sheep and goats lay dead in fields, apparently gored or trampled to death; fences and gates were broken down; the ground was deeply scored in many places as if pawed by a huge beast; even some cottages showed damage to their walls and roofs.

He rode further out into the open heathland and, before long, he could hear it. With a sound like thunder, the ground trembled; Guy knew it to be the thud of hooves. He looked all around him but could see nothing but rough, tussocky grass and patches of scrubby woodland.

From a stand of trees, a flurry of rooks startled upwards and the beast burst forth. It hurled its huge frame towards Guy, the ground rumbling like a rock fall from the impact of vast hooves. Guy could see that his only chance was quick movement and agility, so he drew his sword and jumped down from his horse's back. He had but a moment or two to guess the cow's weakest spot before it was upon him.

The beast lowered its head as it ran, the great horns poised to rip Guy asunder. He waited until the last moment then leapt to one side, striking his sword down hard behind the cow's ear. She faltered, just a little. Guy took his chance and hacked again and again at the same spot before the beast could once more raise her head. The blood gushed from the wound, the cow dropped to her knees and slumped on to her side. Guy swung his sword around and plunged it into her heart. The beast convulsed and lay still, her blood pooling around Guy's feet.

Guy leaned on his sword, breathing hard, trying to regain his composure. After a little while he straightened and stepped through the mire of blood to look at the cow's face. With her wild eyes closed, she looked so peaceful and so mild.

He remounted his horse and returned to Coventry, where Heraud and the earl were waiting. Guy declined the earl's offer of hospitality, saying there was a lady who waited for him. He accepted the prize of gold rings, an ivory cup and chain mail, then took it all to the abbey, asking that they sell it to benefit the poor. The two friends rode home.

GUY AND FELICE WED

Much remained the same; some things had changed. Segward, Guy's father, had died. Rohaud was, of course, older but still straight and strong. Felice had perhaps lost some of her vivacity but she held herself with an undeniable dignity. This time, Guy would have none of whispered, secret conversations. Standing before Rohaud and Felice, dirty and bloodied as he was, he addressed his love. 'I have done many deeds which some would call noble. I have battled tyrants and rescued kings. I come to you now, as you see, fresh from combat where I have freed the people of Dunsmore from a fearsome beast. I will do no more to prove myself. Lady, shall we or shall we not wed?'

Rohaud stepped forward. 'Felice? Surely the answer is yes?'

Felice looked at this man whom she hardly recognised. 'You are much altered,' she said, with more candour than passion. 'But I think I still observe honesty and a sense of honour. Yes, let us be wed.' She offered Guy her hand and he took it in his own. In that moment, she noticed his rough, calloused skin; later she noticed the stain of blood he had left on her palm.

လၥၥ

The wedding was a grand affair, as befitted the daughter of an earl. The feasting and festivities lasted for three days and all, rich and poor, had a share in it. The Abbott of Coventry and the Earl of Mercia were among the guests; it was a great and convivial gathering. Guy and Felice received everyone with smiling courtesy, and if there was any reserve in their manner, it went unnoticed by most.

Finally, Guy and Felice were alone together, as he had for so long craved. This time, less sure of the feelings between them, he had a question that was different in nature from all that he had said before. 'Why, Felice, did you demand so much of me? It seemed that no matter how I excelled, no matter how many heroic deeds I accomplished, no matter how much blood I spilled, it was not enough for you. Why?'

Felice had always known she would have to answer this question, and she was not unprepared. 'You came to me a callow youth, dying for love. How could I make a life with one who so easily gave up the will to live? You were not alone in pressing your suit. Many rich and powerful men would have courted me. Had I married you as you were, my would-be suitors would have made war on you. Any lands you would inherit from my father, they would have wrested from you. They would have killed you. Now, you are a hero. Even here, in the middle of England, we heard news of your gallant deeds. The men who would have fought you and killed you now want to be your allies. Did you not notice who my father had invited to the wedding? Did you not see how those powerful men hastened to lavish gifts upon us and to pledge their allegiance? We now have some hope of living in peace.'

And Guy could not dispute the wisdom or the truth of her words. He was silent for a long time. Then he said, simply, 'There was so much blood.'

GUY'S PILGRIMAGE

Guy and Felice lived together happily enough, for a time. Felice tended her garden, saw to her needlework and busied herself with good and charitable works among the poor and needy of Warwick. Guy assisted Rohaud in the administration of his estates, and all was peaceful for a time.

But Guy began to be restless. He was distracted in his waking hours and his sleep was troubled by a recurring dream. At last, he spoke to Felice of his feelings. 'Felice, I am a haunted man. I cannot forget the needless bloodshed that has dogged me throughout my life. And why? Because I was always driven to prove myself. Men are dead who should now be living because I chose a warlike path. I must attempt some reparation. My soul needs atonement.'

Felice looked at him closely. For some time, she had known this day would come. 'What then will you do?'

'I have thought long about what I should do. I have no desire to leave you; a life with you has been my purpose for so many years. Yet I feel, ever more strongly, that I have a debt which must be paid or I cannot rest. I must travel abroad again, but this time on a pilgrimage. I must visit those places where blood was shed and try to bring some small measure of peace.'

Felice was grave. 'You would leave me? After all you have done for my sake? Now we finally have the life together we have both wanted for so long?'

But Guy would not be swayed from his purpose. He asked Heraud to oversee his interests in Warwick and to look after Felice, and all too quickly he had made preparations for his journey and he was taking his leave. Felice, her face strained but retaining her dignity, kissed him gently and pressed something into his hand. 'In remembrance of me,' she said. He looked into his palm. He held a small gold ring, finely wrought in a curious pattern.

For years, he travelled Europe, seeking out those places where battles and tournaments had been fought and offering prayer and benevolence in any way he could. At long last he began to feel that the debt which could never be paid had at least been acknowledged. Perhaps he could now return to England once more. He turned his face to the west and began the long walk home.

GUY AND THE DANES

In the years of Guy's pilgrimage in Europe, England had been invaded by Danish forces. The Danes had landed in the south-east, and they were well-organised, well-armed and fierce fighters. King Athelstan had done what he could to defend the English people, but his army was less than a match for the warlike Danes. Month by month, the invading forces pressed further westwards across the south of the country while Athelstan saw village after village destroyed, town after town captured.

The Danish army had driven the English troops as far as Winchester; here, in the castle, Athelstan and his men lay under

siege. After several days, the English king climbed the watch-tower to see the hostile forces for himself. He observed with dread his foes encamped all around. He turned away from the scene and made his way down the stairs; he called his marshals and ordered them to assemble the men in the courtyard.

The Danish, for their part, seemed in an almost festal mood. Men sat in groups, talking, laughing, playing games with knucklebones and dice. Here there were fires with cooking pots suspended over them, the smoke and steam rising lazily on the still air. Men strolled up from time to time to help themselves from the vessel, filling a bowl then returning to join their comrades. Some of the soldiers had organised more active games to pass the time; men were running races, wrestling, practising their skills with weapons and engaging in trials of strength. Other men cleaned and polished weapons and harnesses, while still more groomed the horses that were tethered in long lines. Anlaf, the Danish king, seated at ease in his pavilion, both watched his men and glanced occasionally at the castle with the same impassive calm. When he was ready, when his men were sufficiently rested and refreshed, he would act.

Athelstan was addressing his troops. He spoke from his heart. He told the men of his fears for England if Winchester, its capital, should fall: the English people might attempt to fight on for a while, but inevitably they would lose heart and Anlaf would seize the throne. The Danes would rule this fair land and its proud people.

The king asked his men to kneel, and he knelt with them. 'There is but one course left to us. Pray. Pray with me now. God's help is our only hope.'

Every man bowed his head and clasped his hands or folded them over his heart. Athelstan spoke again, his voice low and resonant. 'Let each man say his own silent prayer. For in this time of our direst need, it may be that the humblest among us, who yet speaks truly from his heart, is the one whose entreaty reaches to heaven.'

The silence in the courtyard was profound. Athelstan felt a deep stillness, both within him and all around him, as if the very air was watchful and listening. He became aware, behind his closed eyes, of a faint light approaching. In his inner vision, the light grew in intensity and form as it drew closer until it became, quite vivid and clear, an angel hovering just above the ground, wings outspread, hands stretched forth, face compassionate. The angel spoke simply, 'Go to the north gate. There you will find the one who will save you.'

Athelstan opened his eyes. Before him were the ranks of his men, heads bowed in silent prayer. Above them glowed a light, fading moment by moment but of an unnameable colour whose glory the king would remember for the rest of his life. In the time it takes to draw three breaths, it had gone. Athelstan rose and, like one enraptured, made his way without hurry to the north gate. He would, of course, arrive at the right moment.

He instructed the startled guard to unbar the gate and it swung open to reveal the approach of a man. Seeing him, Athelstan's faith almost wavered. This was one whose lined face and greying hair spoke of a youth left far behind. He wore not armour nor the colours denoting a knight, but a pilgrim's drab robes. He rode not a fine horse; his feet dragged in the dust as he walked. The only weapon he carried, if indeed it could be thus described, was a staff on which he leaned. He entered and the guard closed and barred the gate.

The king knelt and said, 'Friend, we need your help. Please, deliver us from the invading Danes.'

The pilgrim paused. 'I think there is a mistake,' he said at length. 'I came here to ask for bread and water. I am an old pilgrim. The Danes themselves let me pass through their ranks without question; they could see I was no threat to them.'

Athelstan was resolute. He rose to his feet and said, 'No mistake. I was told by one far wiser than I shall ever be to expect you at the north gate. And you came.' And he told the pilgrim of their plight: the seemingly invincible Danish army advancing remorselessly across the land; the siege that would force their surrender or their death; the consequences for England if they failed. And he told the pilgrim of his prayer and his vision.

The pilgrim sighed and considered the king's words for a long time. 'It is true that once I was a warrior of some little renown. Once I was known as Guy of Warwick. But that was long ago. I have chosen a different life and a different path. I cannot go back to what I was. I am making my way homewards to live in peace with my wife.'

The king's expression hardened. 'I will give you a little time to refresh yourself. Then one of my men will take you to the armoury where you can be fitted for armour and you may have your choice of weapons. If you are Guy of Warwick then I am your king and you are subject to my command. No English man will live in peace with his wife under Dane rule.'

Whether Guy would have seen fit to offer a reply we will not know, for at that moment there was a hammering at the gate. The guard drew back a hatch and said to the king, 'A man alone, a Dane. He carries a flag of truce.'

Athelstan nodded his assent; the guard admitted the Dane, who ducked his head towards the king in a cursory semblance of a bow. 'I am sent by Anlaf, King of the Danes,' he said. 'Anlaf would see a little sport. He proposes that our champion, Colbran, engage in single combat with one of your men. He promises that if your man should defeat Colbran, then he and all his forces will leave England and return to our own land.'

'And if Colbran should win?'

'Then King Anlaf will require you, your majesty, to hand over your crown to him and to accept Dane law forthwith.'

Athelstan understood that Anlaf was toying with him; the Dane could, if he wished, simply keep the castle under siege until the king and his men surrendered or starved. Perhaps a swifter conclusion was to Anlaf's liking, and this was a way of achieving it with the least loss of life. Athelstan felt a sudden weariness descend upon him. The fight had been long and hard, and here was a way to end it. He had little doubt that this Colbran would be an invincible fighter, but what choice was there?

'Tell Anlaf I agree,' he said. 'I will send my champion to meet his in combat.'

❧

The day dawned, unseasonably chilly and cloudy. The vast Danish army were seated casually in a wide sweep around the field of combat. They had left space for the English to seat themselves; a mockingly large area, as if to accentuate how small the English host really was. Athelstan's men took up their places, their faces tense.

To a great cheer from the Danes, Colbran strode forth. The man was huge; if not exactly a giant, he was certainly far taller and broader than any other man in either army. He had a sword on a belt about his waist and in his hands he carried a double-headed axe. His armour was light, a breast-plate and leather protection for his arms and legs, as was the style for hand-to-hand fighting. He made a circuit, smiling his acknowledgement of the Danish army, brandishing his axe to further cheers, sneering openly at the English. After a time, the cheers died down and Colbran stood facing Athelstan and his army, his head cocked to one side, as if to say, 'And where is your champion?'

Minutes passed. Then, from behind the seated English, a man appeared. Like Colbran, he was wearing light armour, his belt bearing a sword at one hip and a dagger at the other. He stared straight ahead as he picked his way between his countrymen. There was utter silence.

The man moved almost hesitantly, as if weary of heart and of body. Whispers started up among the Danes: 'Look at that! Is that the best they can do?' 'He's an old man!' 'If it gets windy, he'll blow over!' The man, Guy, ignored the comments and moved on until he stood facing Colbran.

The younger man grinned widely. He looked down at Guy, then lifted his chin and addressed his compatriots. 'It's almost a shame to kill him, isn't it lads?' There was a shout of laughter in response. In an instant, Colbran had hefted his axe and swung it at Guy's head. Guy swayed back at just the right moment and then ducked to avoid the weapon's returning swoop. He darted forward, stabbed at Colbran's thigh with his sword and jumped back out of reach.

The English watched open-mouthed. This weary old pilgrim had transformed before their eyes into a skilled, ruthless fighter. He seemed to have cast off age, fatigue and his reluctance to bear arms and was now entirely focused on the battle. He thrust, he parried, he sprang from side to side, avoiding Colbran's blows while again and again inflicting small injuries. It was like watching a little terrier baiting a huge vicious dog, dashing in, striking, leaping back, all with dizzying speed. Some of the men began to notice, too, that when Guy moved aside from Colbran's blows, he moved more often to the left than to the right so that gradually the Dane was swinging round to the south-east. Two or three saw too that from time to time Guy would glance up at the sky.

Seasoned fighter that he truly was, nonetheless Guy had the weight of years upon him and he began to tire. A breeze had sprung up, blowing wisps of grey hair across Guy's face; he seemed not to have energy to spare to brush them away. Colbran laughed, swung his axe up and brought it sweeping down. Guy once more sprang aside but not quite soon enough; the blade sliced all down his upper arm.

In the moment that Colbran lifted the weapon for the death blow, the clouds drifted from the sun. Heavenly light streamed forth. The Dane took a hand from the axe to shield his eyes. Guy struck, hacking at the man's other wrist. As the axe dropped, Guy snatched it out of the air and swung it round and up to bite into his opponent's neck. The big man crumpled to the ground; Guy swung the axe again and the contest was at an end.

There was silence. The shocking suddenness of the final moments were almost too much to comprehend. Then, the English army were on their feet, cheering, waving, chanting Guy's name.

After a while, when the tumult had calmed a little, a cloaked figure stepped out from among the invading army. He was unarmed and bare headed. He made his way across the field of combat towards Athelstan as the noise stilled once more to silence. He was Anlaf, the Danish king. He finally stood eye to eye with the English king. He said, simply, 'I gave my word.' Then he turned away, to lead his army home.

And all this time, Guy stood by Colbran's body, the younger man's blood pooling around his feet and soaking into the English soil.

☙

That night, there were feasting and celebrations in the castle and all through the town. There was food, there was drink, there was music, there was dancing and much merriment. Towards midnight, a lone figure dressed in a travel-worn robe, leaning on a staff, left the castle and began his long walk to the north.

GUY RETURNS HOME

After days of walking, Guy found himself in countryside that was at once familiar and strange. The lanes, the woodland, the villages that he passed through had changed very little from his memories of so long ago and yet he felt himself to be an intruder. It was almost as if he was in a dream, and he had a growing sense of oddness and unease as he neared his old home.

Towards evening, Guy reached Warwick and Earl Rohaud's manor house. As he approached, he saw that there was a ragged crowd around the steps up to the main door. Coming a little closer, he saw a lady on the steps with a basket over her arm. She was slender and graceful but clearly had left her youth long behind her. She was smiling at the people below her, who stretched out their hands to receive the food she was offering them from her basket. She seemed to have a pleasant word or two for everyone. One by one, the people turned and walked away, carrying in their hands the bread and meat the lady had given them. At last, she stood there alone. She caught sight of the pilgrim watching her from some yards' distance. She smiled again and called to him, 'I have some left, if you're hungry? You would be most welcome.'

Guy was unable to answer. It was his own lovely Felice, and in the twilight she did not recognise him. He shook his head, turned and stumbled away.

He walked for some time in the gathering dusk until at last he found himself on a path near the top of a cliff above the River Avon. At the side of the path, in the cliff face, was a cave and he entered it. There was room to stand upright, and it was deep enough to offer shelter from the worst of the weather. It was enough. He lay down and waited for sleep.

The next day, the hood of his robe raised, he returned to the manor house and this time he joined the group of beggars who waited to receive alms from Felice. She was again pleasant and smiling, with a kind word for everyone. When it came to Guy's turn, he held out his hands and Felice gave him some food, saying, 'Oh! You were here yesterday, weren't you? Have you been on a journey?' Guy nodded and walked away.

He made the cave his home. With food from Felice and water from the Avon, he had enough. Sometimes, he reflected on how contented she seemed, smiling and gentle, helping the poor. He thought about his own life, marked and marred by bloodshed and death. Even when he had tried to atone for the things he had done, he had, on his return to England,

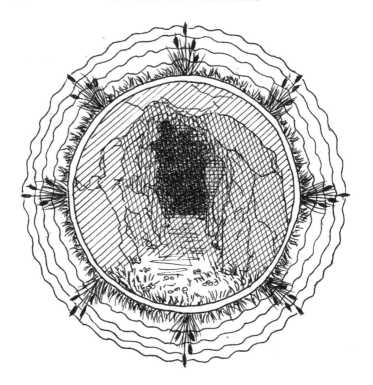

once again been drawn into killing a man. He mused long on the impossibility of making amends for such an act. Death could not be reversed. And the truth of it? He felt most alive when he was killing. He loved to show his skill and strength in battle. He revelled in being the best. But now he would be the best husband he could to Felice. Since death seemed to follow him whether he would or no, he would not reveal his identity to her. He resolved to allow her to carry on living her contented life without him.

Much time passed. Guy became ill with a fever, and day by day he weakened. One day, when he felt his time was near, he watched and waited for someone to pass by his cave. In the afternoon, he heard the patter of small feet; he called the little boy to him. He gave the boy a small object and told him to take it up to the lady in the big house and tell the lady where he had got it. The lady would reward him. The boy nodded and ran off.

The boy ran all the way to the house. As luck would have it, the lady was just coming out on to the steps. The boy ran up to her and put something in her hand. 'The man in the cave gave it to me,' he said.

Felice looked at the small thing in her hand and felt the earth lurch beneath her feet. She reached for the wall beside her to stop herself falling. She looked again into her palm. There was a small gold ring, finely wrought in a curious pattern. She took a few moments to recover herself a little and said to the boy, 'In the cave, you say? Show me where.'

The boy led Felice to the cave in the cliff. She gave him money and sent him on his way. She hesitated only for a moment before stepping inside. There, lying half propped against the cave wall, she recognised the pilgrim who came for alms each day. And, with his hood drawn back, his eyes unnaturally bright, she recognised her own dear husband. She knelt and, with infinite gentleness, took him in her arms. For a long, long time they remained in that embrace, and finally Felice whispered, 'Why? Why did you not tell me you had come home? Why did you not come home to me?'

Guy simply said, 'So much blood.' And that was the last time he ever spoke.

Some say that Felice, in her grief, threw herself from the cliff into the Avon. Others say that she died a little time afterwards. But most agree that Guy and Felice were buried side by side above the cliff in the grounds of what is now Guy's Cliffe House. Their grave is yet to be found, and perhaps, if they are now sharing a peaceful eternity, they prefer it that way.

COVENTRY LEGENDS

LADY GODIVA

The legend of Lady Godiva (or Godgifu, Godifu or Godgife as some earlier sources name her) riding through the streets of Coventry in unusual circumstances is well known, and the story is near to a thousand years old. Here is a version from my own telling:

Haesel the kitchen maid left the manor house by the back door, closing it carefully behind her. Out on the road, she turned towards the town of Coventry and, hitching up her skirt as much as modesty allowed, broke into a brisk trot. She kept up the pace all the way into the centre of the town, across the market square and into a side street. Here, she slowed to a walk. She smoothed down her dress, tidied her shawl and tucked a few escaping strands of hair beneath her cap before stopping in front of a tailor's shop. She peered inside, and seeing young Tom bent over his workbench, needle in hand, she stepped in and flung her arms around his neck.

He started, but his face broke into a wide smile and he caught her round the waist and kissed her. 'Haesel! I wasn't expecting you – it's so good to see you!'

'I can't stay long, Tom, I must be back at work within the hour. I thought perhaps we could walk together a space?'

Tom's face clouded. 'There is nothing I would like more. But you know how it is. So much of the money I earn goes to paying your master's taxes. I must finish this cloak today; I need the pay. And there's more work after that, it'll be an early start tomorrow.'

'I wish Leofric wasn't my master. His lady understands us. I just work in the kitchen, so maybe I shouldn't have an opinion, but it seems to me the two of them work against each other. He takes more than people can afford in tolls, then she comes to the town to give money to help the poorest. But where does that leave you and me?'

'You know what I would like for us.' Tom gazed at Haesel with a sad smile. 'I'm doing my best to make it happen. It's another reason that I work so hard. I wish things would change and we could be together.'

Haesel kissed him gently. 'I know. Let's not give up hope. I'll come and see you again as soon as I can get away,' and with that, she was gone, Tom watching her as she passed out of sight.

⚬✕⚬

Leofric pushed his plate away, drained his goblet and regarded his wife thoughtfully. Now they were alone, there was something he wanted to talk to her about. As good as alone – the kitchen maid had come to clear away the evening meal, but she hardly counted as a person.

He began. 'Look my dear, I know you own a little land yourself but you really have no way of understanding the extent of my responsibilities. Overseeing the whole of Mercia, Coventry's Lord, it's all very taxing and this is why,' he allowed himself a smile at his own wit, 'why I must levy taxes on the people. It's the way of the world.'

The kitchen maid gathered the platters and cutlery into a neat pile, her attention clearly entirely absorbed by this task.

Lady Godiva sighed. They were going over well-worn ground but she felt she had to keep trying. 'It's the people. You should see them. Some of them in the town are working as hard as they can yet they don't have enough left to live on after they pay the tolls. I try to help them but in truth they want to help themselves. Surely you could afford to take less from them?'

Leofric took his time to consider his answer. The kitchen maid, who clearly wasn't very bright, had scooped up the pile of platters in her arms and begun to make her way out of the room when she seemed to notice that the fireplace needed some attention. She dithered for some moments with her burden, looking around for somewhere to rest it down, eventually placing it on the floor by the hearth, where she knelt and began her next task.

Leofric had come to a decision. 'Since you persist in pursuing this topic in spite of my repeated assurances that it concerns matters beyond your experience or understanding, let me make an end of it.' The kitchen maid paused in sweeping the ashes from the fireplace as if considering what to do next. Really, the girl must be quite dim. Leofric continued. 'I am prepared to lift the taxes on the people of Coventry. All except the tolls on horses.'

Lady Godiva gasped audibly. 'Really? You mean it?'

'Oh, I mean it. But hear me out. There are conditions.' Lady Godiva leaned towards her husband; the kitchen maid laid out kindling with agonising slowness.

'Tomorrow, all the people of Coventry must be assembled in the market place, while you are to ride amongst them on your palfrey.' At this, Lady Godiva nodded and smiled.

'And you must be naked.' The kitchen maid, as clumsy as she was stupid, dropped the wood she had been holding and had to gather it all up again. Lady Godiva sat upright in her chair, its back pressing into her own, her face white.

'What?' she said.

'If you ride naked through the town with all the people assembled, then I promise to lift the taxes. But,' Leofric gave his wife a long look. He knew how shy she was. 'I do not believe you will ride through the town with all the people watching you, not naked or even clothed.'

He rose to leave. 'I will send some men to the town in the morning to order the people to assemble, and the people will wait for you. This shows you that I am as good as my word.'

He began to walk from the room, pausing in the doorway. 'Tomorrow. You are to ride as I have instructed tomorrow. Though I do not believe that there is *any* day you will do this.'

As he turned away he said over his shoulder, 'Nor any night for that matter. I mean it about the tolls on the horses though.'

As the sound of Leofric's footsteps grew fainter, the kitchen maid sprang to her feet and ran across to Lady Godiva, taking her smooth hand in her two rough ones. 'Don't worry my lady. The people are on your side. It will be all right. Trust me. It will be all right.'

And so it was for the second time in one day, Haesel left the house and scurried along the road into town, lifting her skirt as high as she needed to run unhampered with all thoughts of modesty forgotten. She arrived at Tom's shop red-faced and breathless, and she hammered on the door. When he opened it, she spoke in a rush, 'I don't have long, I have to get back. Just listen!' And she proceeded, with as much brevity as she could muster, to tell him what must be done.

Lady Godiva spent the next morning pacing her chamber in her night dress. She knew that although Leofric meant his challenge to her as a jest, albeit a cruel one given her modest nature, he was also a man of his word and he would not go back on his promise. So, it was simple then. All she had to do was ride through the town. Without clothes. How can it be, the lady asked herself over and over, that the hardest battles are with oneself? The afternoon began to pass as she struggled with her conscience until finally, her face set, she unbraided her hair and combed it through. She took her long riding cloak down from its hook and wrapped it round her. Alone as she was, she struggled to lift her linen shift over her head while still concealed in the cloak's folds but finally she was free of it.

Holding the cloak tightly closed, Lady Godiva made her way along the corridor, down the stairs and out into the stable yard. In a weak, choked little voice she called for her palfrey to be saddled. After a pause, the groom led the animal to the mounting block. He was observing his feet but, to Lady Godiva's mortification, he was smirking broadly. She stood frozen to the spot and may have remained there – who can say – when the kitchen door flung open and Haesel strode across the yard. She addressed the groom, 'I'll do this. You get on with your work. Go! Now!' The groom scuttled away and Haesel held the horse's bridle. 'When you're ready my lady. Perhaps if you steady yourself with your hand on my shoulder?'

At last, Lady Godiva managed to climb up into the saddle, which was no mean feat with one hand firmly gripping her cloak. Haesel waited at the horse's head as the minutes passed. Finally Lady Godiva nodded to her and she led the horse out of the yard and on to the road. They continued in silence, the girl walking, the lady riding, until they reached the outskirts of the town, where Haesel stopped. 'Should I – would you like me to help you arrange your hair, my lady?'

Godiva bit her lip and fumbled with the fastening of her cloak.

∽

The townspeople had been waiting in the market square all day. Literally all day in fact, since the sun was now beginning to set. Ostensibly, Leofric's men were watching them to make sure everyone stayed, but rather than keeping an eye on the people, they were putting more energy into observing the rota they had hastily drawn up at the start of the day. None of them expected Lady Godiva to take up her husband's challenge so they assumed it would be a long dull watch, necessitating regular refreshment. Having agreed between themselves that it wouldn't make any difference if the landlord of the inn remained at work, and having further agreed that it was probably necessary for two men to keep him under observation at all times, it was simply a matter of dividing the day into hour-long watches.

The men on the last watch at the inn, seeing that the light was fading from the sky, ambled back to the market square to suggest that they all call it a day. They were all agreeing that it was indeed now supper time at home and it would be a shame for it to go cold, when a young woman hurried into the square, a cloak folded over her arm. She shouted, 'She's coming! You all know what to do!' She scanned the faces of the crowd until she saw Tom. She hurried over to him. 'You did tell everyone, didn't you?'

He nodded. 'Even them,' he said, indicating Leofric's men.

Haesel raised her voice. 'Right, now's the time! Cover your eyes!' And all the townspeople did, including the innkeeper, who had come to see, or rather not see, what was going on. Leofric's men stood open mouthed and staring, but Haesel shot them such a fierce look that they hastily covered their eyes too.

The horse, seeming to sense it was taking part in an event of great significance, proceeded at a slow and stately pace. Tom, standing in the crowd, his hands over his eyes, listening to the ponderous hoofbeats, began to worry. Had he spoken to every single person? Did he make them all understand the importance of keeping their eyes covered *for the whole time*? What if someone looked? At last, he could stand it no longer, he had to see if anyone was looking, so he peeped between his fingers – just as Lady Godiva was riding past him. Later, when he confessed to Haesel, he said it was just one peep and he hadn't meant to and anyway, he hadn't seen anything. Only the lady's knee.

☙❧

That evening, Leofric and Lady Godiva sat by the fire together. 'I didn't think my dear, after all these years together, that you could still surprise me.' The man looked at his wife with some wonder.

Lady Godiva blushed. 'I can assure you, no one was as surprised as I! But – you will keep your word, won't you?'

Leofric sighed. 'Have you any idea what this is going to cost me? Yes, as you well know, I will keep my word.' He fell silent and watched the flames with a stony expression.

The lady, herself only a minor landowner and a mere woman, nevertheless understood something of the value of diplomacy. 'I very much appreciate you keeping your word on the people's taxes. I do feel though that I should point out that you were right on three counts.'

Leofric raised his head. 'Really? How so?'

'You said you did not believe there was any day, or night, when I would do the deed. It was nether day nor night, it was twilight. You said I would not ride through the assembled crowd either naked or clothed. I was not clothed, but nor was I quite naked as my hair covered at least part of me. And you said I would not ride through the town with all the people watching me and I didn't. The people were there, but no one was watching.'

Leofric reached for his clever wife's hand; his rueful smile acknowledged appreciation of her wit.

Forty-three years later, after a lifetime of close work, Tom began to think that his eyesight was not what it once was. He wondered, to Haesel, whether it was a judgement on him for the time he peeped at Lady Godiva. Haesel thought perhaps not.

History does indeed relate that there was a time in the Middle Ages when the people of Coventry were free of taxes. Except for horses. There was a toll on horses.

꙳

There have been many versions of the legend of Lady Godiva's ride through the Coventry streets and in the earliest, 'Peeping Tom' does not feature.

In some versions of the story, the people of Coventry all stay indoors to avoid seeing Godiva and in a 1681 painting she is seen riding through empty streets. A man, at the window of his house, is watching her. He is not identified in the painting; some think he could even be a depiction of Leofric looking to see if his wife really does what she says she will. But it is after the creation of this painting that Peeping Tom, the tailor who deliberately watches Godiva's naked ride and is struck blind because of it, begins to appear in the legend. I am gentler with the Tom in my version! Alfred, Lord Tennyson in his poem 'Godiva', tells it thus:

> And one low churl, compact of thankless earth,
> The fatal byword of all years to come,
> Boring a little auger-hole in fear,
> Peep'd – but his eyes, before they had their will,
> Were shrivel'd into darkness in his head,
> And dropt before him.

There are and have been a number of Peeping Tom statues and head and shoulders busts in Coventry, including one that was removed from the old Peeping Tom public house, which used to stand on the corner of Hertford Street. The statue is now to be seen over the entrance to the covered walkway in that same street.

In Broadgate, Coventry city centre, there is the much-photographed life-size bronze equestrian statue of a naked Lady Godiva. It was unveiled on 22 October 1949 and, aside from a reorientation to accommodate changes in the road system, it has remained there ever since.

SAINT GEORGE

Saint George was born in the third century and died in the year AD 303 on 23 April, now celebrated as St George's day. George is the patron saint of England and some say this is unusual because he was the son of a Roman officer and a Greek native of Lydda, and his place of birth was not England but Cappadocia, in modern-day Turkey.

The people of Coventry will tell you a different story.

≈

Many centuries ago, Lord Albert lived with his lady at Caludon Castle in Coventry. One day, the lady came to her husband with the news that she was expecting their first child. Albert was exultant; he had been longing for a son to become his heir. He called his steward and gave instructions that his lady wife was to have servants on hand at all times, and her every need, her every wish, was to be met straight away.

One might imagine that the lady would wish at times for a little peace, quiet and solitude, but she bore the constant attention patiently enough, and the months passed. When her time was approaching, she had a dream so vivid that it awoke her in the dead hours of the night. She dreamed that the new life growing within her body was not a baby at all but a dragon. In the dream she knew with an absolute certainty that the dragon would cause her death.

As she started awake, her heart hammering, she tried to take comfort in the familiar surroundings of her dimly lit chamber, and to remind herself that there was a servant awake and on duty just outside her door. But even in her now wakeful state,

she still felt gripped by the power of the dream. As the baby moved within her, what she had previously taken to be the child's knees and elbows and feet now seemed terrifyingly sinister. Was that a claw? Could she feel the hinge of a wing? She tried to calm herself, but it was no good. She called the servant and asked the girl for a soothing drink; when the servant returned, the lady asked her to remain in the chamber while she tried to sleep. But no more sleep came, not that night nor the next.

Lord Albert, finally noticing how exhausted his wife was looking, asked her what was amiss. She hesitated at first, feeling foolish at being so deeply affected by a dream, then she told him. Albert did not think her foolish. He had been brought up by his mother to believe in signs and portents and this, he felt, was momentous.

Albert called his steward and said, 'I want the watch over my wife to be doubled. Let no one whom we do not know come near her.' The steward nodded.

'And I must consult with one who has exceptional wisdom,' Albert went on. 'Call my knights. I must know which of them can help me find a person of subtle cunning.'

Albert chose the wisest of his knights, and the two men set out that same day. The knight knew of a woman reputed to have a mysterious power; she was said to live in a distant forest. It was two days' ride, and in all the time the two were journeying together, Albert said but little.

The forest was dense and dark, but the path through it was wide and clear. The two men had little choice but to follow it, and Lord Albert had the strong sense that he was being purposely led. After some hours, the land, though still thickly wooded, became more hilly and rocky and the path began to wind around the base of a craggy cliff. The men halted in front of a huge ragged fissure in the rock face. It was barred by intricately wrought gates of a metal that neither man could name; beyond the gates were wooden doors banded with the same strange metal. Both gates and doors appeared locked, and there was no key. Albert said to the knight, 'What should we do?' and the knight could only answer, 'This is beyond me. I think we have to wait.' After a moment, the knight continued, 'This, I believe, is the dwelling of Kalyb, a most cunning and powerful woman. From what I hear, she will not see us until she is ready.'

No birds sang, no stream chuckled, no breezes rustled the leaves. In the distance there was a brief howling roar. It seemed to Albert that it was a sound half human, half monstrous. The horses started as, at their feet, a snake hissed and slithered away. From above their heads came a harsh grating cawing sound. They looked up to see, on the branch of an oak, a raven. It carried a trumpet, hanging from a scarlet cord around its neck. It seemed to be waiting, its head cocked to one side, its eyes bright and knowing.

Albert urged his horse on few steps until he was under the branch; by standing in the stirrups he could just reach the trumpet. The raven remained still, apparently waiting for Albert to take hold of the trumpet, then it ducked its head out of the loop of cord. Yet before it flapped away, it pecked hard at the lord's hand, drawing blood as scarlet as the cord.

Albert raised the trumpet to his lips and blew. Albert blew again, and a third time. He and the knight watched the gate and the door behind it. Surely they would open. They did not.

Then a voice spoke. It seemed to be a woman's voice, though deep and resonant. It was as if the very rocks were speaking.

'Sir Knight.'

'Yes!' Albert's chest was tight. 'I am Lord Albert. I come to seek your counsel.'

'I know why you are here.'

'May we enter and speak with you? If you know why we are here, you will know it is urgent.'

There was a pause. Then: 'No, it is not. The urgency has passed. Albert, you should have stayed at home with your wife. Here is the only counsel I can give you: you have a son, most strangely born. He will become the champion of all England. In time, you will see the truth of my words. But now, you should return home. I say again, you should never have come here.'

'But my wife's dream? What of that? Tell me what it means!'

The voice was silent, and it spoke no more. At length, Albert glanced at his companion, who shook his head. Albert hung the trumpet by its scarlet cord on the twisted metal of the gate. Both men turned their horses' heads towards home and for a long time neither man spoke. Lost in thought as they both were, neither of them noticed a nondescript old woman cradling a bundle in her arms as she walked on the path towards them. Nor did she speak to them as they passed.

⚬⚬

Albert's lady had watched his departure from her chamber window, her faithful maid by her side. No sooner had Albert passed from view than the lady gasped and pressed her hand to her side. The maid, all concern, said, 'Is it the baby my lady? Shall I send for Lord Albert to be called back?'

The lady shook her head. 'Just help me to the bed. When he returns, I will have a new baby to show him.' She could not know how wrong she was; the one who did know had already set out on the journey towards Caludon Castle.

The birth pains came frighteningly fast. The best doctors and midwives had already been called to the castle in preparation for this event, and they made sure that the lady was never left unattended. It did her little good. Her labour went on and on, all day and all night until she was beyond exhaustion and the baby was no nearer to being born. Three doctors and the most experienced midwife withdrew to an outer chamber to hold a solemn conference.

'We cannot save them both,' said the senior doctor. 'I wish Lord Albert was here. I do not want to take this decision without him.'

The midwife spoke, her face drawn. 'I have seen this before. If we do not act quickly, it will be too late for them both.' She paused, and glanced towards the lady's chamber. Even through the heavy door, they could hear how ragged her breathing had become. 'Lord Albert is not here to make the decision. His lady must decide for herself.'

The four stood in shocked silence. At last, the midwife led the way. At the door, she asked the doctors to wait and let her speak to the lady alone. Truth be told, it was a conversation they were only too glad to avoid. The midwife gently opened the door and went in.

When she returned to the waiting doctors, she was wiping her red-rimmed eyes furiously with the back of her hand. She took a few moments to steady herself and said, 'She says you are to save the baby.'

After that, it all happened very quickly. The doctors prepared a draught that would free the lady of pain. It would free her of life, eventually, too, if the operation did not kill her first. The midwife held her hand from the beginning to the end and as the baby emerged into this world, the lady slipped into the next.

It was a deeply strange moment. The grief they all felt at losing the lady contrasted sharply with relief at the birth of a healthy boy, turning to wonder as they all saw the marks on his body. On his chest, as clear and distinct as if it had been drawn with a fine pen dipped in scarlet ink, was a dragon, perfect in every detail. And on his arm was a cross; that too was precisely outlined and blood red.

While the doctors went into a huddle to have an urgent discussion about how none of this was their fault, they had acted for the best and were blameless, the midwife was busy.

She had never seen a birth or a boy like this before, but she was wise enough to know that powerful forces were at work, and that powerful forces attract powerful opposition. She gave the baby to the maid with instructions to wash him and dress him, and she sent another servant to fetch the steward. When he arrived, she told him that the most trusted servants must be chosen to care for and watch over the baby at every moment of every day, and a wet nurse was needed straight away – he must send to the village to find one. The steward, although accustomed to taking orders only from Lord Albert, saw the gravity of the situation and did as he was told.

☙❧

A stranger arrived at Caludon Castle. She was unbidden and unnoticed. She was indeed nondescript, looking unremarkable in every way, but more than that, she had a way of not even avoiding attention, but somehow slipping beneath it. She made her way silently to the castle kitchen and, when the cook was attending to the fire, made some additions to the food and drink intended for the baby's maids and wet nurse. She then passed through the corridors and up stairways until she stood outside the baby's room. She stepped back into a shadowy corner, where she could observe the door. Soon, a servant arrived with a tray laden with plates of food and a silver jug. The servant was admitted and reappeared shortly afterwards with the empty tray.

The stranger knew she did not have long to wait. After a few minutes, she entered the room to find all of the women sleeping, with only the baby awake. She scooped him up and concealed him beneath her garment while she made her way

out of the castle once more. A guard was on the outer door; she had almost passed him, unseen, when a group of servants hurried up the steps and bumped into her. She half-turned so the baby would not be startled and cry out and thus lost her balance a little, knocking into the guard. He looked down with surprise, seeing her for the first time. But there was nothing to cause him concern, only a harmless old woman.

'Good evening to you, old mother,' he said as she went on her way. She did not reply. She could not; she had left her voice in a cave in a dark forest.

Lord Albert returned home to the most terrible news. He sent his men to search the countryside for the baby; periodically they returned but with nothing to relate. He himself went into a sharp decline, grieving for his wife and for the loss of his baby son, and he was not in his right mind for many months. When at last he began to recover a little, he resolved to spend his life searching for his son until he found the boy or until death overtook him. He never found his child.

⚭

In her cave in the forest, Kalyb the enchantress cared for the baby. She called him George; why would she not, for her acutely clear sight told her that was his name. Years passed and George grew to be a youth; his noble nature shone through in spite of his strange upbringing and he thirsted for honourable adventures.

Kalyb was the sworn enemy of true nobility, yet having stolen the child she gave him the best care of which she was capable, and indeed now he was approaching manhood she found herself falling in love. It was just as the enchantress's feelings for George reached their height that he became determined to escape. She, sensing his restlessness, became unsure of the charms she had put in place to keep him captive and she conjured a strengthening of the guard upon him.

She tried to think of every art and diversion she could offer him, but George wished only for deeds as befitting a knight. Kalyb, for all her skill as a sorceress, could cast no spell that would make George genuinely love her or even admire her, and it was this very thing, which she could not bring about by artifice, that she most desired. She began to think that perhaps she could win his heart by another means. She offered to make for him an impressive show of her power.

George considered her offer. He reasoned that he might in some way exploit the situation to gain his freedom. He said, 'Madam, let us be direct. You have an amorous intention towards me. It would perhaps not be distasteful to me to fulfil your wishes.'

Kalyb narrowed her eyes. She had always taken care to appear to him as a beautiful young woman, but she suspected he might somehow be aware of her true form and nature. 'You mock me?' she asked.

'I can understand that you might think that. But if I am to be a husband to you, I must be of sufficient power and standing to match your own influence. Appoint me governor of your cave and your domain. And you can satisfy my curiosity: who am I? Truly?'

The second request was easily fulfilled. 'You are George, son of Lord Albert, high steward of all England, and his lady. Your mother died to give you life. Your father died searching for you.'

'My mother died for me? What is her name?'

'I do not know. It was long ago, can it matter now?'

The anger that George felt at Kalyb's dismissive words must have showed in the sudden flush of his cheeks and the flash of his eyes, but he said nothing. A dish best served cold.

Kalyb had already turned away, bidding George to follow her. She led him deep into her cavern through narrow passageways until there was a sudden opening out and there before them were sunlit rolling hills and, its entrance not a hundred yards away, a castle that appeared to be wrought of some strange metal. George looked for guards or servants but there appeared to be none, and he followed Kalyb through the castle gates and into the stable yard. There, saddled and bridled as if waiting for their riders, were seven fine horses. The finest of these was Bayard, a horse, Kalyb said, of great intelligence and magical powers. 'He is yours,' she said simply.

George turned his head, listening. 'Do I hear voices calling for help? Far away voices?'

'No, there are no voices, it is only the wind.'

From the stable yard, Kalyb led George into the armoury, where she fitted him with armour. 'It is of the purest Lybian steel,' she said. 'I have added enchantments that will prevent any weapon from piercing or even bruising it.'

She took a sword from the wall and handed it to George. Its balance was perfect and it fitted his hand like it had been made for him. 'This is the sword Ascalon,' said Kalyb. 'It will shatter flint. The hilt is imbued with such magic that when you are holding it or when it hangs from your sword belt no violence or evil craft can be wreaked upon you.'

George accepted the sword and buckled it to his belt. He listened again. 'I think I can hear voices.'

'No, there are no voices. It will be some enchantment lingering from long ago.'

Kalyb led the way into the castle courtyard. It had four sides; three of the sides were the castle apartments. The fourth was a wall of solid rock. She said, with some pride, 'Here is a place that some may find horrific. Within this rock are the bodies of all those who have died at my hand. But if you are strong enough to bear it, we may pass through and you will see that beyond are wonderful riches. Why don't you prove to me how brave you are? Take my wand and open the rock.'

'Yes, I will. But you say there is no one calling for help? I do hear voices.'

'I told you, it is the wind, and old lingering magic. Now, will you take this?'

She handed him a silver wand. The moment he touched it, he felt a strong urge to drop it, so strangely abhorrent did it feel. But he held on and struck the rock. A fissure appeared, and for a moment George saw sights that made him flinch and almost recoil, but he did not hesitate. He pushed Kalyb inside and struck the rock again. It closed and he saw the witch no more.

He was silent for a few moments, his head tipped to one side. Then he turned towards the faint sound of voices. His feet led him to a heavy door on one side of the courtyard. He used the wand to open it, then made his way down the stone steps beyond. He found himself in a dungeon with precious little light. He could just make out another door, and again the wand opened it.

Six men were inside the cramped stone chamber. George gestured for them to follow, and soon they all stood blinking in the castle courtyard.

In the armoury, as the men furnished themselves with weapons, shields and mail, they each told a similar story. Every man present was a warrior on the side of right and justice; Kalyb had a hatred of nobility and chivalry and so she had lured them to the castle and kept them captive. What would have become of them had George not released them was unthinkable.

'In the castle stables are horses fitted to a knightly quest,' said George. 'Let us ride out together in search of adventure!'

And thus the seven companions began their journey together. Every day they rode on towards their destiny; every night they made their encampment and six of the company told stories of their adventures and exploits. George, having not yet accomplished any valorous deeds, listened with fascination. They travelled in this way for thirty days until they reached a broad plain. There, in the distance was a tower; they rode towards it and as they approached they saw that it was made of brass and traced with strange designs. From the foot of the tower led seven pathways. The company took this as a sign, and, every man bidding each of the others a loving farewell, they set out, one to a path.

George missed the warm fellowship, but he was glad that at least he had the company of his horse, Bayard. Together they travelled for many days and at last found themselves in Egypt. There was a town a little way off, but as night was falling George stopped at an isolated hermitage. He called out, and the hermit appeared and ushered him inside, leading Bayard to an adjoining stable.

The hermit offered George food and drink and as they sat at their meal together, his manner was courteous but guarded and sombre. George enquired whether anything was troubling him.

The hermit said, 'I must advise you to leave this place as soon as it is light. There is a monster, a dragon, that has laid waste to much of the land. At first, the people placated it with a sheep each day, but when there were no more sheep, we were desperate. A decree from the king has forced the people to sacrifice one of their maidens to the dragon every day. Lots are drawn, so the dreadful fate of the young women is at least fair. Now, the king's own daughter has been chosen; she is to be sacrificed to the dragon tomorrow.'

George was incredulous. 'Can nothing else be done? Must young women be fed to this beast? And now it is the turn of the princess – surely this cannot be!'

The hermit said, 'The king tried to plead with the people of the town. He tried to buy his daughter's freedom with silver and gold, but the citizens would not be bribed. Like all the others before her, she is to be left outside the dragon's cave at dawn. Her fate is certain.'

'But has no one tried to destroy this creature?'

'Yes, many have tried, and died in the attempt. The beast is immensely powerful and its scales are stronger than any armour.'

George said no more on the matter, but he resolved to do his utmost to rescue the princess. He refused to take the hermit's bed and instead lay on the floor to sleep for a few hours. Well before dawn, he arose, donned his armour and took his leave of his host.

As George approached the town, he saw in the pre-dawn light a sombre procession on its way to the nearby hills. A young woman stood in a mule-drawn cart, like one going to her execution. A few townspeople walked alongside. George rode up and joined them. He spoke to the princess. 'Do not fear, good lady. I am come to slay the beast; it will not trouble you this day or any day.'

The princess turned to look at him, her expression not afraid but weary. 'It has been this way for so long. Others have tried, but the dragon cannot be killed. You are so young. Do not lose your life in a hopeless quest.'

George smiled and said no more, but simply rode alongside her.

At the cave, the princess willingly stepped down from the cart. The townspeople began their journey back to the town with barely a backward glance. This daily horror, thought George, had become all too commonplace. He sensed not callousness in those who left the young woman to her fate, but a hopeless resignation.

He turned to her and told her quite firmly that she must stand aside so as not to hamper him in his battle. She did as he said, sheltering behind a rock, still close enough to see what happened.

Before long, the dragon began to emerge. First, wide nostrils scenting the air, then the huge head, its reptilian eyes fixing on George and Bayard. Seeing the size of the creature, George rode a little way away and released his lance from its socket in the saddle. The dragon was now entirely out of the cave, its body enormous, its outstretched wings creating a powerful wind, its long tail thrashing.

George levelled his lance and urged Bayard on. They hurtled towards the dragon and, more by luck than judgement, just avoided the down sweep of the vast head. The steel tip of the lance met the scaly chest and the wooden shaft shattered. Bayard veered away and circled, galloping once again to the attack. George heard a voice – could it be the horse? – 'Draw your sword! Now!' He pulled Ascalon from its scabbard as Bayard with perfect timing dodged under the leathery wing. George plunged his sword up to the hilt into the unguarded flesh and the dragon stiffened and fell with a thunderous crash.

All was still. It was hard to believe, after all the noise and tumult, that it was so suddenly over. The princess emerged from behind the rock. She looked at the dragon and she looked at George.

'I expect,' she said, 'that my father will want me to marry you.'

George looked at the princess. 'I expect,' he said, 'he will.'

That is one version of how George came to slay the dragon. I have drawn from a number of sources and from my own telling, but it owes a lot to an account written by Richard Johnson in 1861, *The Seven Champions of Christendom*. I could not find a name for George's mother; George's anger at Kalyb for not knowing it is my own invention. There is an addendum to the story, after the point where I leave it: George meets again with the other six champions and all seven repair to Caludon Castle, where they stay together for nine months, overseeing the building of a fine monument over George's mother's grave.

Johnson records the names of the six champions rescued by George. They were: St Denis of France, St James of Spain, St Anthony of Italy, St Andrew of Scotland, St Patrick of Ireland and St David of Wales. Quite a company.

The name of the princess saved by George from the dragon was Sabra. In other versions of the story, George saves the City of Coventry and the daughter of the English king from the dragon. He marries the king's daughter and they have a son who later becomes known as Guy of Warwick.

Caludon Castle was built in stone following the Norman invasion. Prior to that, it was a Saxon stronghold. One wall remains and can still be visited; the castle fell into ruin in the nineteenth century and, as was often the case, the stones were taken away for local building work.

George's horse is named Bayard in this version of the story. Whether this is the same famed Bayard that was owned by Renaud (or Rinaldo) in The Four Sons of Aymon, a *Chanson de Geste*, I do not know.

Once, on the road between Bidford on Avon and Wixford,

near Alcester, an elm tree stood, known as Saint George's Elm. The story goes that Saint George was buried there and the tree grew from a stake (presumably elm) that was driven through his body. Why Saint George should be buried by the side of a road and why he should have a stake driven through his body is not explained. The tree was reputed to bleed if its bark was cut. The tree is unfortunately no more.

DOOMED LOVE

Here are a few stories that really don't turn out well. If you're in the mood for something less than sweet, then this is the chapter for you.

LITTLE COMPTON

I touch on the English Civil War in the chapter about Edge Hill. In the seventeenth century, William Juxon was Bishop of London. He was an ardent Royalist and supporter of Charles I, at whose execution he was seen to weep. He inherited a manor house near to St Denys' church at Little Compton from his brother and it was to that place he retired. No longer allowed to practise his faith or tend to the spiritual needs of his human flock, he had little to occupy his days. After his death, his voice was still heard echoing in his home, preaching to his invisible Anglican flock as he was forbidden to do in life.

William Juxon's story can be seen as one of doomed love – his love for the monarchy – but there is more to his story. He was deposed as Bishop of London under Oliver Cromwell but at the Restoration of the Monarchy in 1660, Charles II appointed him Archbishop of Canterbury. The disembodied voice heard at the manor house was, it seems, from an earlier, unhappy period of his life.

ଓ

If we move forward two hundred years or so, the fourteenth-century church of St Denys has been extensively restored.

There is a vicar in post, but this story concerns his curate, Mr Drane.

Mr Drane was a conscientious young man who could be relied upon to assist the vicar in every way required of him. He helped the vicar in his visits to the sick and the poor of the parish, he led the Sunday school and organised the mothers' meetings and – his favourite task – he readied the church for the Sunday service.

Early each Sunday morning he would make sure that the church had been properly cleaned and the lectern dusted, that the hassocks and prayer books were in place on each pew and the choir stall was perfectly polished, with the hymn books placed neatly on the shelf. Especially, the best hymn book with the red calf binding must be placed at the centre of the choir stall where Miss Fielding would sit.

The choir would arrive early, before the rest of the congregation, and Mr Drane would wait to welcome them as they came to the church in ones and twos and threes. Miss Fielding, a popular young lady, often arrived with friends. She would come strolling up the church path, chattering gaily to a girl on either side of her and sweep past the young curate, occasionally bestowing the briefest of flashing smiles on him before returning to her animated conversation with her friends. She would take up her usual place in the choir, pick up the hymn book that had been placed there so lovingly, and sing like an angel. She was, indeed, known as 'Birdie' Fielding because of her naturally beautiful singing voice.

One Sunday, Miss Fielding arrived alone. Mr Drane saw his chance and tried to muster all his courage as she approached him.

'Good morning Miss Fielding!' He knew his smile was too bright. 'Lovely day!'

'It is indeed, Mr Drane,' Birdie Fielding murmured as she made to go past him into the church.

'Er! I was thinking, next Saturday, if the weather is fine!' He knew he was talking too fast. 'I have some free time, possibly you would care to take a walk with me?'

'Possibly,' she said, with an amused smile as she walked on.

Saturday came and the weather was fine. Mr Drane was unable to eat his breakfast and tying his bootlaces and buttoning his jacket had become puzzlingly difficult. At last he was ready to leave the house, his face flushed, a mixture of hope and fear in his eyes.

At Miss Fielding's house he rang the doorbell and tried to arrange his face into a suitably pleasant expression. The door was opened by a smartly dressed young maid. Mr Drane stumbled so much over his request to see Miss Fielding, the maid had to ask him to repeat it.

'Oh,' she said, 'I'm afraid Miss Fielding is on an excursion with her young man. Was it about the choir, sir? May I take a message?'

Mr Drane muttered a few words that even he failed to understand and hurried away.

Some weeks passed. Miss Fielding requested an interview with the vicar. 'I am betrothed,' she said with a bright smile, 'to Captain Brandon of the Grange.'

The vicar offered his congratulations, thinking that the captain was indeed a good match – dashing, handsome and very wealthy.

'I wonder, could we set a date? Next month would be ideal,' said Miss Fielding.

As the vicar opened his appointments diary, Miss Fielding stretched out her hand to stop him. 'Oh, but I thought, as he is *so* involved with the choir, wouldn't it be lovely if Mr Drane conducted the service?'

And so it was that Mr Drane, his face unreadable, married Miss Fielding to Captain Brandon. After the exchange of rings, rather than instructing the captain to kiss his bride, the curate himself leaned towards her and, so gently, kissed her cheek.

The congregation, with the happy couple in the lead, made its merry way to the Grange and the wedding breakfast. Mr Drane was not seen at the meal, nor was he seen for the rest of the day. It was the parish clerk who, as night was falling, became anxious about the young curate. He found, at last, that Mr Drane had never left the church that day. The clerk discovered him in the belfry. Hanging from the bell rope.

MARGARET AND ALICE CLOPTON

Clopton House is a mile north of Stratford-upon-Avon. It has now been divided into luxury apartments, but it was the Cloptons' family residence for centuries, first is recorded in 1221.

⚬⚭⚬

Love today is no doubt little different from love through the ages, and five hundred years ago, Margaret Clopton of Clopton House was indeed in love.

Eyes shining, she went to her father to tell him she wished to marry. He listened with some sympathy until she mentioned the name of her lover, then his face clouded with anger. It is not recorded why Margaret's father would not accept the match; perhaps he was too poor, or of the wrong social class, or the son of an enemy. We do not know. All that is known is that Mr Clopton forbade Margaret to wed or even see this young man, and no pleading or entreaty would move him.

In other similar stories, the young couple run away together, but in Margaret's case this did not happen. Perhaps she would not agree to it, or perhaps her beloved could not muster the nerve to carry out such a plan; whatever the circumstances, the young lovers saw each other no more.

Distraught at the loss of the only man she believed she would ever love, Margaret left her bedchamber one night when all was still. She stole out of the house, into the grounds and to the well. There, whether swiftly and resolutely or hesitantly and with misgivings we do not know, she flung herself in and she drowned.

The well was covered over, and the stone over 'Margaret's Well' could still be seen in recent times. Poor Margaret's ghost has been seen by the well, and in her bedchamber where she spent her last night, and if you go to the site of the well you may hear her whispering, whispering.

℘

Some years later, Alice Clopton – she may have been Margaret's sister – was betrothed, and on this occasion her father approved of the match. It was the day before the wedding and all the final preparations had been made. Alice at last retired to bed to spend her last night as a single woman.

At some time in the night she was abducted from her room and no one realised she had been taken until her kidnapper was riding away with Alice on his horse. It is not set down how this was accomplished. Did she not call for help? Why did no one in the house awaken until it was too late? She must, I think, have been drugged, perhaps by a bribed servant.

Her husband-to-be was alerted, and he lost no time in mustering a party of stout fellows to ride with him in pursuit. The kidnapper was seen to have taken the road north towards Birmingham so the rescuers knew the direction to go, though the man now had a long head start on them.

The chase went on for hours, and the kidnapper's horse must indeed have been stout hearted, for he was carrying two and he had run for 25 miles before the pursuers had him in their sights. It was near to Deritend bridge that the fugitive, glancing behind him, saw the party of men riding furiously towards him and gaining ground. He must now abandon his plan, no doubt to hold Alice for ransom, and make good his escape by lightening the horse's load. As he crossed the River Rea by Deritend bridge, he flung Alice over the parapet of the bridge and into the rushing waters below.

Alice's betrothed leapt from his horse and dashed into the water to save her, but while he was able to pull her body from the cold river, her life had already departed and there was nothing anyone could do.

Following a desperately sad funeral, Alice's betrothed could no longer face the world, and he eventually became a hermit, making his home in a cave in Blackstone Rock overlooking and high above the River Severn. In time, the hermit became renowned as a healer; he had developed skills in curing ills of both body and mind.

One day, many years later, a man came to see him. The man told the hermit that he was troubled in mind over a crime he had committed a long time ago. He had abducted a young woman and then, to save himself, he had thrown her into a river where, he later heard, she drowned. The hermit listened quietly, then said, 'Let us step outside for a moment. I like to look down at the river while I think.' The man followed the hermit to the ledge above the Severn. The hermit put his arm around the man's shoulders. 'I pray for both our souls,' he said, and with that, he leapt into the river, dragging the man with him. They both drowned.

EDGE HILL

The Soldier's Prayer

O Lord, thou knowest how busy I must be this day. If
I forget Thee, do not Thou forget me.

THE YOUNG SOLDIER

He had been sleeping fitfully; anyone watching would have seen
his muscles twitching, his hands grasping, his face grimacing, all
accompanied by a low, panicky murmuring. Then he became
more still, his body relaxed a little and his eyes opened.

He turned his head from side to side, taking in the dreadful
scene that surrounded him; it had not after all been just a
dream. He did not know how he could have slept at all, fully
clothed on the cold hard damp ground, but he must at last
have dropped off from exhaustion.

Other men lay on either side of him. Some of the faces he knew. A few had their eyes closed. None was breathing. Their blood was drying in the weak early morning sun, hardly risen over Warmington church.

The young man's name was John and he was a soldier in the parliamentary army. His memories of the day before were hazy and jumbled: the parliamentary cannonade, roaring missiles at the enemy, the artillery on his own side but terrifying; the endless sea of thousands upon thousands of men; pikes bristling, pointing sharply into the sky; the hill before them and above them with rank upon rank of cavalry and foot soldiers all waiting for the order to charge.

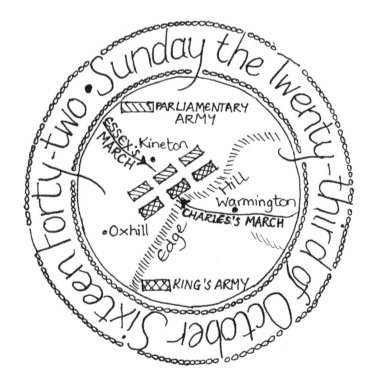

He did not remember the blow to his head that had both felled him and saved him. A Cavalier had struck him as he rode past, his aim spoiled by the speed of his mount's flight. John knew no more until the battle was over, when he came round to see only the darkening October sky above him, his head too sore to move. How long he lay like that through the cold night he did not know, but restless sleep finally claimed him.

He cautiously propped himself up on one elbow. His head throbbed a little, but a more urgent problem was his thirst. He could not remember when he had last tasted water. Taking his time, he got on to all fours and from there, like a child trying to stand on two feet for the first time, testing his balance all the while, he stood up. He looked around him and was more shocked by what he saw than he could express. On all sides Cavaliers and Roundheads alike lay dead. The countless bodies were all men who had been alive only the day before.

But desperate physical need is a powerful thing, and when John's gaze fell upon a water bottle strapped to a man's belt, he staggered towards it. Unbuckling it and raising it to his lips, he found it to be fresh and clean tasting. He drained the bottle, then fastened it to his own belt for future use, reasoning that its owner would have no more use for it. The dead man had been a Cavalier, with extravagant clothes and rings on his fingers. John gazed at the rings for some time. If the man had no use for his water bottle, then no more would he need gold or gems, and after all, he was one of the enemy. After a little hesitation, John knelt and pulled three rings from the man's hands and as he did so, he noticed the jewelled pin that held the man's cloak in place. He unclasped the pin and then slipped all of the jewellery into the bag slung over his shoulder. Straightening up, he found himself looking around, scanning the other bodies, seeking anything that glinted or sparkled.

He moved from corpse to corpse, taking a ring here, a necklace there, a brooch there. Each time, it became an easier thing to do. Each time, it felt less like theft and more like a transaction: 'You don't need this, I do, so I'm taking it.' He began to rifle through pockets, taking only the more valuable coins, aware that whatever he took he would have to carry. His bag filled.

As the sun appeared above the church, John walked from the field of battle and down the hill towards Kineton. There he entered the first inn he came upon, and the staff, up and about and preparing breakfast, gathered around and asked for news of the battle. John gave them a dramatic account that was partly invented, as he had been unconscious most of the time, but it pleased his audience who, horrified and fascinated, hung on his words and drank in every detail. The party was abruptly broken up by the landlord, who strode in and demanded to know why no work was being done.

John hastily apologised for interrupting the staff in their duties and explained that he was a soldier from yesterday's battle. The landlord nodded his understanding, and his eye fell on John's shoulder bag. 'Bessie!' he called to one of the staff. 'Bring a bowl of water and a clean cloth. This man needs his head bathed and bandaged.' While that was being done, the landlord instructed one of the men to prepare a private room where John could wash and rest.

'First, though, you must eat and drink,' he said to John. 'You must be hungry. Then, when you have rested we will talk some more. I think I can help you.'

John thanked the landlord and, after his meal, was only too glad to be able to wash the sweat and dirt from the day before from his body and to lie down on a comfortable bed.

It was dark again when he awoke, and by the sounds coming from the bar below, the inn was doing a good evening's trade. John picked up his bag and made his way downstairs to join the company. As soon as the landlord saw him, he hurried over and ushered John towards a table in a secluded corner. 'I want to have a quiet word,' he said. 'It is greatly to your advantage.'

John sat down with the landlord and accepted the tankard of ale that a servant brought over. He waited for the other man to speak.

'I see that you have certain items in your possession,' the landlord began, gesturing towards John's bag.

John cut him short. 'What do you mean? You see nothing at all. Have you been going through my things while I've been sleeping?'

The landlord was unruffled. 'Not at all, lad, no. I don't need to. It's just common sense. A man does not go on to a field of battle with a heavy bag over his shoulder. Therefore, when did the bag become heavy? How was the bag filled?'

He took a long draught of his ale, letting John consider the weight and import of his words. He went on. 'You may know, or you may not. The Earl of Essex – he's your leader, isn't he? Well, Earl Essex has issued a decree that there shall be no looting on the battlefield, no robbing the fallen. So when you're caught with that bag,' he nodded at the item in question, 'you are going to be in a lot of trouble. There will be a court martial. Neither you nor I know what the penalty may be, but we can both hazard a guess.'

John shifted miserably in his chair. Denial was useless. 'What can I do then?'

The landlord smiled kindly. 'Well, isn't it obvious? You leave the bag here with me and I will hide it in my good oak chest. After a few weeks, when everyone's attention will no doubt be taken up by another battle in another place, you come back here and claim it.'

John was young, but he was not stupid. 'And what's in it for you?'

'One tenth of the value of everything in the bag. It's the best deal you're going to get.'

John saw that it was indeed not a bad deal, and it was a good deal better than being caught with valuables looted from the battlefield. He agreed, and, having first filled his pockets with coins from the bag, he handed it to the landlord.

The next day, he left the inn and walked out into the Warwickshire countryside, intent on losing himself for a few weeks.

It was in fact six weeks later, on the evening of the first of December, low on cash but with a good warm coat on his back, that he returned to the inn at Kineton. He went in to where three men were sitting drinking and he greeted the landlord, who stared at him blankly. John, already feeling uncomfortable without quite knowing why, said in a low voice, 'I've come for my bag.'

The landlord said, more loudly than necessary, 'What bag? Who are you? I don't know you!'

John wondered for a moment if the landlord was being discreet and he was talking that way for the benefit of the other men, but when he nodded to them and they rose as one, fists clenched, John finally saw how he had been tricked. He opened his mouth to speak, then thought better of it, turned on his heel and went out into the street.

He started walking, not noticing where he was going, trying and trying to think of a plan to get his bag back. He was passing a printer's shop when a man stepped out of a deep shadowy doorway. He was tall and broad with a close-fitting cap and John could just see in the dim light that the man's teeth were bared in a semblance of a smile.

'That was a bad business, was it not?' said the man.

'The battle you mean? Edge Hill?' said John, peering at the man's face, wondering if he should be recognising a comrade.

'Well,' the man said, 'I suppose you could call that a bad business, depending on your point of view. But no, I was meaning something rather more immediate. Your bag. Your treasure.'

John frowned and took a step back. The man continued, 'I could help you get it back. In fact I could promise you will get it back.'

'And why does it interest you? What do you have to gain? What would I have to give you?'

'A trifling thing, no more. Something I expect you don't even know you have and that you will never miss. Only your soul, that's all.' The man bared his teeth again.

John took another step back. 'Look, I don't know who you are, but you're not funny, all right? I don't know what you think you know about any property of mine, but if anyone has stolen from me then I'll take it to court. I don't need your help. Just leave me alone.' John turned and began to walk away, marvelling at his own words. It had not occurred to him until that moment that he could let the court settle it, but now he had said it, it seemed to be the only thing to do.

The stranger called after him, 'Have it your own way. But you'll see me in court. Make no mistake about that. You'll see me in court. Look for my red cap.' But John was already striding away.

It was only three weeks later, just before Christmas, that the case was tried at Stratford-upon-Avon Court of Record. With the last of his coin, John had employed a lawyer to help him at the hearing. The magistrate listened as John accused the landlord of stealing his bag; he did not specify the contents, only that there were items of value, and he certainly did not mention how he had come by them.

The magistrate called on John's lawyer to produce witnesses or evidence, and the lawyer brought a servant from the inn to the witness box. It was Bessie, the girl who had washed and bandaged John's wound.

'Did you see this young man arrive at the inn?' the lawyer asked, indicating John with a wave of his hand.

'I did, sir,' said Bessie.

'When he arrived, did you notice if he had anything in his possession?'

'Yes, sir. He had a heavy bag over his shoulder.'

Did you see this same young man as he left the inn?'

'Yes, sir, I did' Bessie replied.

'And when he left, he was carrying the same bag?'

'No sir, he was not. He wasn't carrying a bag at all.'

'You are sure?'

'Yes, sir, quite sure. It looked heavy, and it had a way of swinging against his hip that I noticed when he arrived. I'm certain that bag was not on his shoulder when he left.'

'Thank you Bessie. You may go.'

Bessie stepped down from the box and left the court, catching John's eye with a smile as she went.

Then it was the landlord's turn in the witness box. At that moment, John noticed a tall, broad man in a red cap making his way along the side of the court. He approached the landlord and stood just behind him. John looked around at the magistrate and the court officials. Surely one of them would tell the stranger to step away? But none of them seemed to notice.

John's lawyer began his questioning. 'The court has heard that this young man arrived at your inn with a bag and left without it. We can only guess that you have either sold the bag and its contents, or it is still in your possession. Which is it?'

The landlord puffed up his chest. 'If he is careless with his things, what business is it of mine? I can't be expected to watch over the possessions of all my customers!' The man in the red cap bared his teeth in a manic grin.

The lawyer pressed on, 'Come now, admit it! You have this young man's bag, haven't you? Or you have the coin made by selling it!'

The landlord's face grew stubborn. 'I do not have his bag. I did not sell anything of his. If I am not telling the truth, may the Devil take me!' The stranger did not wait to be invited twice. He stepped forwards, his long arms snapped around the astonished and terrified landlord's waist in an iron grip, and the two of them disappeared, seemingly through the floor. When the court officials ran forward, there was nothing to be seen; no gaping chasm, not even a split in the floorboards. Just a pair of cloven hoofprints scorched into the wooden floor.

The landlord never did reappear. Bessie searched in his good oak chest and found the young soldier's bag, which she returned to him. John thanked her warmly and then said, 'What about you? Will you lose your job now there's no one to run the inn?'

'Well that depends,' said Bessie. 'If there was a good strong young man with a little coin at his disposal to take it over, then I imagine there would still be work for me to do. That's right, isn't it?'

And it was.

THE SPECTRAL BATTLE

A story is told of Sir Edmund Verney, standard bearer to King Charles. In the way that battles were conducted in those days, the standard, the ceremonial banner of that army, was more than ostentation. It could be a rallying point in the chaos of hand-to-hand fighting and it was a beacon of hope for the troops. It would have taken considerable courage to carry the king's standard, since the bearer would render himself a target; the enemy could gain a great symbolic advantage by capturing the flag.

As the battle raged at Edge Hill, Sir Edmund was indeed the focus of hostile action when a number of Parliamentarian soldiers accosted him and wrested the standard from his grip, making off with it into the midst of their own men. With no regard for his own safety, Sir Edmund rode in pursuit. Sword in hand, he fought his way fiercely through the knot of men, gaining ground towards his goal until he faced the man with the standard – and won it back.

At some later point in the battle, the standard was again lost and at great personal cost to Sir Edmund, as we shall see.

There lived in Kineton the vicar, a Mr Samuel Marshall, and a Justice of the Peace, Mr William Wood. On a cold mid-December morning in 1642 they each awoke to strange news. Mr Marshall's maid told her master and Mr Wood's coachman told his of how it was all around the town that a small party of men had witnessed an unaccountable sight the night before.

When Marshall and Wood met each other in the street shortly afterwards, they were both bent on the same mission: to hear an account of the previous evening's events first hand. The town was buzzing with the news and so the men involved were soon found.

The party repaired to the front room of an inn. The vicar and the JP ordered refreshments for them all and settled down to listen to the men's story. This is what they were told: the men had been walking home from their work. It being winter, the sun had set at about four o'clock and as they crossed Edge Hill plain in the Vale of the Red Horse, it was dark and they had to pick their way with care. All at once, each man was frozen to the spot as they heard ghastly sounds: at first drum beats vibrating in the air all around them then, soon after, shouts and screams as if they were in the centre of an unseen place of carnage. Movement appeared in the sky, faint and flickering at first but growing in awful clarity until it was plain that they were witnessing the battle that had taken place on that spot less than two months before.

They saw soldiers, many very young, with weapons that only some of them seemed confident of using. There were cavalrymen charging at each other and trampling over the foot soldiers. Men with pikes were inflicting terrible injuries on their countrymen. Soldiers were shot with muskets and hacked with swords. Cannon roared and drums thundered, all but obscuring the shouted commands. All the time there were shrieks from the wounded and groans from the dying. It all seemed at once near but distant; real but unsubstantial; and frightening in the extreme.

The men stood and watched because they had no choice. To a man, they felt unable to move until the whole hideous spectacle had played out. They became aware, as the sights and sounds of the battle finally abated, that they had been transfixed for three hours and had witnessed the conflict from start to finish.

Mr Marshall and Mr Wood listened to this account without interruption. It was clear to them that, fantastic as the story was, each man was completely sincere. Their white faces, staring eyes and hesitant voices persuaded their listeners that they at least believed the tale they were telling. Marshall and Wood thanked the men and left to discuss between themselves what should be done. They decided to see for themselves.

That night, Mr Marshall and Mr Wood, wrapped in their warmest clothes and accompanied by a few others, made their way to Edge Hill, each man carrying a lantern. They did not have long to wait. The light from their lanterns soon appeared dimmed by the blaze of activity in the sky as the events, exactly as described to them, were played out. At the same time, the people of the town were awoken by the sound of drums and trumpets and the cries of the fallen. No one now was in any doubt as to the truth of the first witnesses' statements, but the town was in turmoil, many fearing that these visions were visitations from hell.

Mr Marshall the vicar set out for Oxford to where King Charles was stationed to report the events. Charles sent 'six gentlemen' to Edge Hill to investigate the matter. These gentlemen interviewed those who had witnessed the spectral battle and they also saw it for themselves. They were most startled to see that they not only saw the battle played out in full, but they also recognised some of the combatants: Prince Rupert on a white horse courageously leading a charge; and Sir Edmund Verney, cut down at last on the battlefield.

The six gentlemen made their report to Charles. The manifestations continued, becoming something of a talking point among the population, with two pamphlets that were published in January of 1643: *A Great Wonder in Heaven* and *The New Year's Wonder*.

All this time a feeling was growing, especially amongst the people of Kineton, that the ghostly armies were seeking to draw attention to a wrong that needed to be put right. Perhaps, as the ground was rough and dotted with furze and other bushes, there were still men lying dead on the field but without a Christian burial.

A party of volunteers went out that January to search the frozen ground. Several bodies were recovered, and after they were properly buried the strange celestial manifestations ceased.

Since that time, there have been occasional ghostly sightings. Some people believe that the battle is re-enacted every year on 23 October, and the Edge Hill battlefield attracts a number of ghost hunters annually. Over the years, Prince Rupert has been seen leading a cavalry charge down the hillside towards the Roundhead troops. A white horse wanders the field on the eve of battle, looking for his rider, whom he will carry to his death the following day. Sir Edmund Verney was not only killed in battle; his body, it seems, was never found. He lost the royal standard, gained it again but finally lost it, the hand holding it being severed from his arm. It is said that his ghost wanders the battlefield endlessly searching for the hand that still clutches the banner.

Estimates of the number of casualties following the battle vary from 1,500 to 6,000. There were too many to bury individually and mass graves were dug, known as Little Grave Ground and Great Grave Ground. C.J. Ribton-Turner, writing in 1893, noted that the grass growing over the graves was a brighter green than in their surroundings. A copse of trees grows on one of the graves, and some say that dogs will not enter it.

Although fewer phantoms have been seen at Edge Hill as years have gone by, it is still a place of interest. Anyone wishing to visit, however, has to content themselves with viewing the field from a distance since it is now owned by the Ministry of Defence and it is fenced off.

LONG MARSTON

This story is not, in fact, about Edge Hill, but it forms a nice addendum since it concerns an incident at the end of the Civil War.

Charles II's soldiers met the Parliamentarians at the Battle of Worcester on 3 September 1651. Charles was then but 21 years old. His troops were soundly defeated by Cromwell's army and he had to flee for his life, pursued by a party of Roundheads.

He was not without friends, and he was making his way south to sanctuary at the house of one George Norton. He was travelling with Norton's sister-in-law, Jane Lane, and Charles was, of course, in disguise, as Will Jackson, servant to Jane Lane. From Worcester they had travelled to the village of Long Marston, 5 miles from Stratford-upon-Avon, and there they found a friendly house to give them shelter for the night.

The owner of the Long Marston house knew who it was who was sheltering under his roof, and he also knew that the fewer people who were aware of the young man's true identity the better. So the house servants were kept in ignorance of the fact that they had a royal personage among them, and indeed one with a price on his head.

'Will Jackson', as befitted a servant, was sent to work in the house kitchen under the direction of the cook. She looked him up and down, decided she didn't think much of him, and pointed to the meat-jack. 'There,' she said, 'wind that. Take care, it's good meat.' And she busied herself with making pastry.

Will nodded and began to turn the meat. Before too long, the cook sniffed deeply. 'Are you burning that meat? Didn't I tell you to take care?' She hurried over to find her fears realised; the meat was beginning to spoil.

'I'm sorry, mistress, but I don't know about meat,' said Will.

'You don't know? What is that supposed to mean?'

'I come from a poor family,' he said, 'We don't hardly ever have meat.'

The cook's eyes narrowed. Was he giving her some sauce? She took in his innocent expression, concluded that he was and clouted him hard on the side of his head.

The history of England might have been very different if she had not, for just at that moment, the door from the outside yard opened and in strode three Roundheads. They watched the scene for a second, laughed to see a kitchen boy getting his just deserts and went on their way.

Charles, of course, eventually escaped to the Continent and was later crowned king of England.

ILMINGTON
NOODLEHEADS

There are many towns and villages across the country where 'noodleheads' or, less politely, 'fools', are said to be found. Ilmington is not one of them. Rather, and more unusually, it is from Ilmington that the stories originate; it is more often the case that such stories do not all originate from one source. The Ilmington noodlehead stories are all about the residents of a nearby village, Ebrington, or Yebberton as it is sometimes pronounced. What the Yebbertonians have done to deserve it I do not know – but then, as far as I can see, noodlehead stories are always undeserved. So, biased and unfair as they no doubt are, here are some noodlehead stories from Ilmington.

THE WHEELBARROW

John had a small farm in Yebberton. Truth be told, it was tiny, more of a large back garden and hardly worthy to be called a farm. Yet John kept chickens, he had an area fenced off for his pigs, he had a cow (which sometimes had to be taken along the lane to enjoy the lush hedgerow grasses and flowers, so small and bare was its field) and he grew vegetables. He even had a little field where he grew barley.

John did not seem, to those who knew him well enough to be entitled to an opinion, to be a fool. He managed his little plot of land very well. He had found out through trial and error that barley was more tolerant of the local climate than was wheat, so barley was what he grew. There was grain enough for his own bread, for the pigs' feed and some left over for the chickens. His vegetables met his own needs and allowed him to swap with neighbours as well as to sell the remainder at the market from time to time. Sometimes he had eggs and cheese to sell too. All in all, it was hard to see how anyone could have done better.

Because of the small size of the land he owned, John had no use for a cart. Indeed, he would hardly have had room for one. Instead, he employed a wheelbarrow. It was just the right size to carry food for the pigs or chickens, to transport sheaves of barley into his shed, to load with manure to fertilise the earth and to carry cheese, eggs and vegetables to market. We can only hope that the implement was thoroughly cleaned between those last two operations. So useful was John's wheelbarrow that it began to wear out, and John could see that there would be a need to replace it soon.

John counted the coins that he had saved in a box under his bed. Though it would be not at all true to describe him as miserly, he was certainly careful with his money, and he found that he had enough put by to easily afford a new barrow. As luck would have it, one of the best local barrow makers sold his wares in Campden, less than 3 miles away, so one sunny morning John set out on the Campden road, a song on his lips and coins in his pocket.

He arrived before midday, and allowed himself the pleasure of strolling through the market place, taking notice of what was for sale and for how much. He came to the wheelbarrows, and there were several to choose from. John began chatting to the barrow maker, who told him of the virtues of each. One was made of ash, which was a strong resilient wood, as was chestnut, but neither was as good as the oak barrow, which was strong, resistant to warping and far less likely to rot than the other two woods. John ran his hands over each barrow, just as if he was considering buying a horse. The oak barrow was by far the best, with comfortable handles at a perfect height for John, skilfully made joints and a strong iron band encircling the wheel. It was also the most expensive. John decided to walk another circuit of the market while he considered the purchase.

On his return, his mind was made up. Economy was all very well, but false economy was just that, false. John chose the oak barrow. He paid and began to wheel it away. As he came to the edge of the town, he stopped to admire his purchase. He was concerned to see that the iron wheel rim had picked up dust and dirt and little scrapes from its journey so far. It seemed to John to be wrong that the wheel of the beautiful new barrow on which he had spent his hard-earned and carefully saved money should suffer any wear before he had even got it home.

He thought for a little while and then sighed. There was nothing else for it. He picked up the barrow in his strong arms and began to stagger home. It could reasonably be presumed that the homeward journey was no longer than the outward, but to John that day it seemed very much longer. But the end of the journey finally came and John proudly placed the barrow down on his own land, where the wheel would at least be scuffed and scraped in pursuit of the purpose for which he purchased it.

And that is the story. The question remains, was John a fool? I know what I think; what do you think?

THE CHEESE IN THE ELM

As I write, there are very few elm trees growing in Warwickshire, or anywhere else in England, since most of them were killed by disease decades ago, but this story takes place in a time when fine tall elms were a common sight in hedgerows all across the land.

It was a fine night, and several Yebberton villagers were making their way home from the inn. They were perhaps not as inebriated as they could have been, but nevertheless it is fair to say that they had left the inn in a different condition from that in which they had entered it.

As they passed a field, one woman lifted her gaze to the starry sky. She stopped, her mouth falling open in wonderment. When she had recovered herself a little, she called to her companions who had walked further on. 'Look!'

The others stopped. 'What?'

The woman pointed up into the crown of an elm. 'There, up in the tree. It's caught in the branches.'

Her friends retraced their steps and looked to where she was pointing. Sure enough, there was a round object that did look as though it might be entangled in the tree's upper limbs.

'What is it?' said one.

'I think it's a cheese,' said the woman. 'It's certainly the right shape.'

There were murmurs of assent. 'It's a beauty,' said a man. 'It's all round and silvery. That probably means it's got a good crusty rind. Probably nice and mature.'

The others saw that he was right. A round, shiny, silvery thing, what could it be but a cheese? The obvious thing to do was to get it down from the tree. Everyone stood in silence, pondering the issue. After several minutes, someone said, 'Anyone got a ladder?'

This was met by universal head shaking. More silence. Then, the man who had asserted the maturity and good rind of the cheese had an idea. 'We don't have a ladder but we do have chairs and tables. Let's all go and bring our chairs and tables out here, and on the way, knock on your neighbours' doors and get them to bring theirs as well.'

This was accomplished, but not without much struggling, bumping of shins and falling over. But, at last, a number of tables and chairs were assembled at the foot of the tree and the task of piling them up began. Well, they weren't stupid. They stacked the larger, heavier tables at the bottom, followed by smaller, lighter ones, then (there being two men at the top of the pile who were doing the stacking) the chairs were passed up one by one and the men arranged them into a more or less secure structure.

There being little room at the top, one of the men climbed down, leaving the other – he was the 'crusty rind' man – to stand aloft and try to reach the cheese. He couldn't. He called down to the now quite sizable crowd, 'I need more furniture.'

'We haven't got any,' called back several spectators.

Crusty rind man was undaunted. 'Well, pull some out from lower down the pile and pass it up!'

I have already mentioned that these people were not stupid. The man realised that pulling a tier of furniture out from the pile would make it less stable, and he reached for a branch above his head and wrapped his arms around it to steady himself. 'I'm ready!' he called.

It took a little time for two people to climb on to the table at the bottom and pull out a smaller table higher up, so the pile did not collapse straight away. But when it did, it was

sudden. One moment, crusty rind man had his feet firmly planted on Mrs Taylor's old but sturdy kitchen chair, the next, he was swinging by his arms from a worryingly high branch.

'Help!' he said. But the others had observed a strange phenomenon and were absorbed in puzzling over it. In the last hour or so, no one could say exactly when, the cheese had moved away from its moorings and was now, quite inexplicably, hanging in mid-air with no visible means of support.

And the man? One fact about elms that I did not mention at the start is that they are reputed to hate mankind because of their tendency to drop large branches without warning, to the detriment of anyone passing beneath. Or indeed of anyone swinging from the branch at the time.

YEBBERTON CHURCH

St Eadburgha's church was named after the granddaughter of Alfred the Great, and its oldest parts date to the thirteenth century. It has many remarkable features and is well worth a visit. None of these facts has much bearing on this story; we just need to know that there was a church.

༺ꙮ༻

An old tramp was in the lane, passing the church, when he observed a group of parishioners standing in the churchyard with the parson, deep in conversation. Every now and then, they would all cock their heads to one side and peer at the church, then shuffle a few feet to the left or the right and stand on tiptoe or crouch down, as if in search of a better view.

The parson put his hands on his hips and frowned. 'It could be.'

A florid-faced man, dressed rather better than some, puffed up his chest. He was the church warden and was inclined to be generous in the matter of sharing his opinion. 'I think it most definitely is,' he announced. Some of the others murmured their assent.

The parson nodded, his face grave. 'Well, yes, I suppose it is. What shall we do, I wonder?'

The church warden took charge. 'Let us assess the facts. We all agree that the ground on the south side of the church is slightly higher than the ground on the north side. We also agree that a church is supposed to be on high ground.' He narrowed his eyes as he stared at the church and then at the bordering green turf. 'It is my estimate that we need to move the church six feet to the south. That should do it.'

The parson brightened considerably at this. 'Well! That's what we shall do then!' He turned to the church warden, knowing that he could rely on him to appoint himself foreman. He was not disappointed; the man did not hesitate in instructing all those present to take off their jackets and lay them on the grass near to the south side of the church.

'That is so that we will be able to see how far the church has moved. Now, everyone round to the north side, you too, please, parson, and we'll push.'

At this point the reader may be wondering why the parson, as an educated man, would agree to such a scheme. All I can say is that an Ilmington teller of this tale might well point out that he was in fact a parson, but a Yebberton parson, and that explains everything.

Well, everyone did indeed go round to the north side. They placed their hands on the church wall and braced themselves and, on the churchwarden's signal, pushed hard. Their faces reddened, their muscles strained, their breath came in gasps. At last the church warden allowed them to stop. They all straightened up cautiously and eased their aching backs, then made their way round to the other side of the church to see how far they had progressed.

As a man, they stopped dead. No jackets were visible! They had obviously pushed the church so far that all their jackets were now underneath it. They jubilantly shook one another's hands in mutual congratulation.

Just out of sight, further down the lane, a tramp was hurrying on his way, the pack over his shoulder bulging with jackets.

YEBBERTON CHURCH TOWER

St Eadburgha's church has a tower. It's the oldest part of the church, and as towers go, it is probably fair to say that it's not as lofty as some.

One day, the parson, the church warden and some of the parishioners were standing together in earnest contemplation of that tower.

'I quite like the colour of the stone,' ventured the parson, 'but I admit you might have a point,' (this to the church warden), 'it does look a little grubby.'

'Well, that's my opinion,' said the florid-faced man. 'We really must keep up standards. I think we should paint it.'

One of the group brightened. 'I know where I can get hold of gallons and gallons of whitewash, cheap.'

Everyone nodded. Whitewashing the tower would be a great improvement. But the parson hit upon a snag. 'How do we decide what colour whitewash to use?'

Everyone nodded again. It was a good point. The choice of colour was crucial to the upkeep of appearances. Then the man who knew where to get hold of gallons and gallons of whitewash had an idea. 'I'll go and have a look. I'll see what colour it is and come back and tell you all.' And off he went.

While the others were awaiting his return, they again fell to contemplating the tower. One said, 'I've seen taller.'

The church warden bridled. 'It might not be very tall, but it's very solid. I'm sure it's a very fine tower.'

'Fine, yes,' agreed the first man. 'But short. Squat, even.'

The parson, observing the church warden's face flushing an even deeper shade than its usual crimson, hurried to pour oil on troubled waters. 'Perhaps when we find out the colour of the whitewash,' he said, 'we will see that it's an expansive sort of colour. It will in all probability make the tower look taller. Not,' he continued in haste, 'that it needs to.'

The church warden opened his mouth to speak, but another of the group was quicker off the mark.

'I know – Farmer Jones has a huge manure heap. I'm sure he could be persuaded to donate some to the church. We could spread it all around the foot of the tower, it'll help it to grow.'

This idea met with general approval, so the one whose idea it was went off to speak to Farmer Jones. The parson smiled weakly. He had a vague feeling that the whole scheme was getting out of hand but he couldn't quite explain to himself why or how. The church warden was trying to decide whether or not he should take offence at this latest development. The two of them were still deep in thought when the whitewash man made his return, perched on top of a number of cans which were in turn piled up in a donkey cart.

He waved, beaming. 'I checked. It's white! That'll do, won't it, white goes with everything.'

The church warden, thinking he should take charge, detailed several of the waiting group to unload the whitewash and carry it over to the tower. They were still complying with his instructions when Farmer Jones' wagon, pulled by a large black and white horse, rolled into the churchyard. 'Where do you want it?' called the farmer.

The parson stepped forward, feeling he should wrest at least some of the initiative from the church warden. He thanked the farmer and directed him to dump the load of manure at the base of the tower. This was accomplished with some manoeuvring, swinging round and backing up of the exceptionally good-tempered horse, and the farmer went on his way.

Now there was another issue to consider. The pile of manure was perilously close to the cans of whitewash; this could be remedied in the short term by removing the cans to a more distant location, but the problem of how to combine the manuring and the painting operations remained. The group of parishioners stood, once again deep in thought.

One man's face suddenly brightened. 'Ha! Look at it this way! If we paint the tower then manure it, when the tower grows, we shall have to paint it again, 'cos the new growth will be the original colour.' The rest of the group, being resident in a rural location, knew this to be true. New growth may sometimes be a little paler before the sun had ripened it, but it was essentially the same colour as that from which it had grown.

The man went on, 'What we should do, is manure it, let it grow, then when it's reached its final height, we can paint it.'

All agreed that this was the logical thing to do. Even the church warden, who was put out that he hadn't come up with the solution himself, could find no fault with the plan. The cans of whitewash were duly moved into the churchyard shed, and the manure was spread around the base of the tower. The farmer had been generous, and the layer of manure reached nearly a foot up the wall.

Over the next few weeks, gravity and the occasional shower of rain did their work and the fertilizer gradually settled. There was a faint but definite crusty tide mark to show the previous level, and this was noticed one day by the church warden. He went to find the parson, who was dead-heading some roses on the far side of the churchyard.

'Parson! My idea worked – the tower has grown! Now for the next stage of my plan. I'll call a few helpers and organise the painting!'

The parson, either through wisdom or resignation, simply smiled and nodded.

THE ROOF

Old Tommy tucked the stubby pencil behind his ear and held up the scrap of cardboard, the better to see the magnificence of his drawing. To be fair, in terms of artistry, it was rudimentary, but it served its intended function. It was a plan. The roof had, obviously, to be the right width, and that dimension was included in the pencilled notation; the height had caused old Tommy far greater pause for thought but in the end he thought he had reached the best compromise between the proportional beauty of the overall design and the length of the wooden poles likely to be easily acquired. He comforted himself with the thought that Rome wasn't built in a day and neither was it built with unavailable materials.

Tommy was keen to get started straight away. Unfortunately, it was still daylight, and the greater part of his plan would need to take place under cover of darkness. He strolled down to his favourite place in all the world: the duck pond on his little farm. He sat down on a large stone at the edge of the pond – the upper face of the stone was kept remarkably clean of moss by the regular application of the seat of Old Tommy's trousers – and fished in his pocket for the scraps he always kept for the ducks. He scattered the scraps and the sleek birds clustered round his feet, pecking at the ground and keeping up a low squabbling quacking.

Old Tommy remained with the ducks, perfectly contented, until the sun had set and darkness began to fall. Then he rose and went to his shed. He emerged with a large, ragged-toothed saw and set out for Squire Pearce's woods. Once there, he made his way to the first of the boughs that he had secretly marked in daylight. His criteria were strict: the wood must be in good condition with no decay; it must be of a sufficient size to be cut to the required length; it must not be too big to drag back to Tommy's farm; and it must be growing low enough on the tree to allow Tommy to cut it down while standing on the ground.

The project was, of course, not completed all in one night. The fallen boughs had to be trimmed of their branches before being dragged along the woodland path, and Old Tommy had to be careful only to use his saw when the gamekeeper was likely to be at the local inn. But eventually, Tommy had his roof beams. Now for the uprights. The Squire was having much of the fencing surrounding his land replaced, and consequently there were piles of chestnut fence posts, waiting to be put in their places, all along the border between the squire's land and Tommy's. The thing to do was to only take one or two from each pile, then the purloinment would not draw attention to itself.

At last, Tommy had all the materials assembled. The construction of his grand design took a further few days, what with knocking in the uprights to a sufficient depth, fixing them all together with smaller branches cut from the large boughs and nailed horizontally, hauling the roof beams into place and securing them with a combination of scavenged nails and lengths of woodbine, making an unscheduled extended canopy to shelter Tommy's favourite sitting-stone and finally, with rushes gathered from the squire's lake, thatching the lot in a makeshift and amateur but effective effort.

When it was all finished, the last rush stem pegged into place, the bindings checked and tightened and the nails all knocked securely home, Old Tommy made his weary way up to his little farmhouse for his evening meal. He was too tired to cook anything, so he placed a hunk of bread and some cheese on a plate and put in his pocket two small sweet apples that he had collected from a tree of the squire's that was so near to the fence as to be practically on Tommy's land. He took his pipe and tobacco pouch down from the mantelpiece and strolled back to the duck pond. He sat down on the stone and surveyed his handiwork. He now had cover from the sun and the rain, and so did the whole pond and therefore, so did the ducks.

Old Tommy ate his bread and cheese, then crunched his way through the two apples. If enough is as good as a feast, then simple food enjoyed is as good as a banquet. He took out his pipe, filled the bowl with tobacco, tamped it down and took his time lighting it. He smiled. The sky darkened, and after a while there was little to be seen but the glow of Tommy's pipe as he drew upon it, and little to be heard but the gentle chuntering quacks of the ducks at his feet.

This story, like the story of John and his wheelbarrow, is generally told to show up Old Tommy as a noodlehead, a fool. Was he, though?

BIBLIOGRAPHY

Alexander, Marc, *British Folklore, Myths and Legends* (Stroud, UK: Sutton Publishing, 2002).

Atkins, Meg, *Haunted Warwickshire* (London, Robert Hale, 1981).

Bloom, J. Harvey, *Folk Lore, Old Customs and Superstitions in Shakespeare Land* (London: Mitchell, Hughes, and Clarke 1929).

Bradford, Anne, *Haunted* (Redditch, UK: Hunt End Books, 1992).

Mee, Arthur, *Warwickshire Shakespeare's Country* (London: Hodder and Stoughton, 1936).

Neuburg, Victor, *The Penny Histories* (Oxford: Oxford University Press, 1968).

Palmer, Roy, *The Folklore of Warwickshire* (London: B.T. Batsford Ltd, 1976).

Folklore, Myths and Legends of Britain (New York: Reader's Digest, 1973).

Smith, Betty, *Ghosts of Warwickshire* (Newbury, UK: Countryside Books, 1992).

Smith, Betty, *Tales of Old Warwickshire* (Newbury, UK: Countryside Books, 1989).

Swift, Eric, *Folk Tales of the East Midlands* (Nashville, TN: Thomas Nelson and Sons Ltd, 1954).

Westwood, Jennifer, *Albion A Guide to Legendary Britain* (London: Granada Publishing, 1985).

Westwood, J. and Simpson, J., *The Lore of the Land* (London: Penguin, 2005).

https://archive.org/details/TheSevenChampionsOfChristendom/page/n29/mode/2up

www.catholic.org/saints/saint.php?saint_id=280